Time to say Goodbye

Barbara Carmichael

PAPER MISSILE
NIYOGI BOOKS

Published by

NIYOGI BOOKS

Block D, Building No. 77,
Okhla Industrial Area, Phase-I,
New Delhi-110 020, INDIA
Tel: 91-11-26816301, 26818960
Email: niyogibooks@gmail.com
Website: www.niyogibooksindia.com

Editor: Arkaprabha Biswas
Design: Nabanita Das
Cover image: Mitchell Ng Liang an

ISBN: 978-93-89136-37-1
Publication: 2020

Printed at: Niyogi Offset Pvt. Ltd., New Delhi, India

This book is dedicated to the memory of
Tarun Singh Inda,
my dear friend and brother.
And it is a gift to his family: his wife Manisha,
daughter Rudrakshi and his son Rudraveer.
His brother Shakti, wife Poonam, daughter Riya and
son Mahipal. And of course, to my dear Indian Mamma,
along with loving thoughts of Raj, Tarun's father.
To my Indian family, from Barbie with love.

Contents

Prologue

'This will keep you safe,' you said as you pressed the ruby into my hand. At that time, I did not realise the significance of your gift. But from the moment we met, you were my protector. No matter where I was on my travels, you always checked in on me—with a phone call or a message—just to see if I was okay. I felt I could go anywhere in India and you were beside me.

Seeing India through your eyes taught me so much. From you I learnt patience, understanding and the appreciation of simple things. I miss you, Tarun.

I often wonder what it was in that first meeting that led us to such an improbable friendship; in time, you became like my brother. I like to call it destiny. And never in my wildest dreams could I imagine that anything would happen to you.

I remember the moment. It was 1:00 am on a hot summer's night. I'd been tossing and turning, so I came downstairs and decided to check my emails and found your cousin had posted a photo of you on Facebook. I moved further down the screen, and there was another photo of you, and another. It was that photo I took on the night we went to the City Palace in Udaipur for Holi. Under your photo it read, 'We regret to inform you that Tarun has passed…'

I went into panic, frozen to the screen. I looked again, read again, reread the date: 2 December 2014. I collapsed back in my chair. 'Please God! No! Not Tarun! my dear friend, Tarun.'

I decided to call you. Ridiculous, I know. Of course, there was no answer. By the time I phoned the number of your hotel, I was shaking, crying.

'Kishan, it's Barbie.'

'I'll get Shakti,' was all he could manage. His voice was hollow. My heart pounded the walls of my chest as I waited, hoping to wake up from this nightmare. Your brother came to the phone. He cried when he heard my voice.

'There are no words, Barbie,' he sobbed. He was right. There were no words. I knew then that I would have to come back to you in Udaipur—I would have to come to say goodbye.

But I didn't know if I could do this without you, my friend. I didn't want to do it without you. My love of India came from you, Tarun. You are my India.

And then, I thought of your family. I needed to be with them…

I hold my ruby tightly as the plane touches down. I press it between my fingers, feeling its sharp edge. As I walk into arrivals I look through the glass where you would stand and wait for me, but you're not there. I think that by some miracle you'll be there, waiting. I watch for my luggage on the carousel and feel my eyes welling. I look through the glass again and I can see your daughter, Rudrakshi. She waves. She is so much like you. She runs to me as I come through the door and throws her arms around me. She has grown. She's getting tall like you.

Your friend Deepak is there, along with Mahipal, Shakti's son. Deepak hugs me. 'He's still here,' he whispers. 'Just ask him and he'll show you.'

It's quiet in the car from the airport. Rudrakshi holds my hand. 'I have to be brave for Mummy,' she tells me. You would be proud of her, Tarun. I squeeze her hand gently and look out of the window. Trucks, rickshaws, motorbikes stream past in the endless current, that is India. It comes to me then, as I squint into the dusty orange light, that I will go to the lake. That's where I will find you. That's where I'll be able to say goodbye.

Memories, 2006

It was January. The weather was cool; the tranquillity of the early morning pierced only by the rhythmic drumming of washing paddles as local women pounded their laundry on the ghats by the lake. A dog barked in the distance. It was the first time that I had seen the Taj Lake Palace, seemingly floating on Lake Pichola. It looked like a painting.

I had only just arrived in Udaipur, and Tarun had booked me into a quaint little haveli called Kankawa.

'The rooftop overlooks the lake,' he told me as he dropped my bags at the reception. 'Come and see.' His face beamed. 'Come. This way.'

He beckoned me to follow up the steep, narrow stairs; their treads worn smooth. He turned around, checking whether I was behind him. His long legs made the climb effortlessly. He was on the rooftop before me, waiting, his arms outstretched towards the view.

'And just for you Barbie, I have organised for the lake to be full.' I laughed, and then as I stepped up beside him, I breathed out a sigh that seemed to go on forever. I was transfixed.

'I knew you would love it,' he said quietly, watching me.

A flock of birds circled the palace and a tiny boat bobbed its way across the mirrored surface, the engine hardly audible.

'It's like something out of a fairytale.'

Looking across the water, I could see the reflection of the mango trees on the other side and the Ambrai restaurant where we had dined the previous year—its tables and chairs placed on the foreshore.

That had been my first trip to India, at a time when most of Rajasthan had been in drought. It was extraordinary to think that then we had been able to walk across the parched bed of the lake to the palace and stand on its very foundations. Now, here I was again, and the palace had regained its majesty and the city its soul. Canopied boats drifted past, with guests from the palace momentarily reliving the romantic life of maharajas, laying back on silk cushions while light muslin curtains billowed in the breeze. I didn't want to miss a single moment of such a vision. I felt that if I blinked, it would all disappear. Peace surrounded the Palace on the lake, and I felt it flow through my body. I'd known I had to come back, and now I knew why.

Maybe, it was my escape from the safe, beige north shore of Sydney to the mass explosion of colour that drew me back. Before I left Australia, I had cooked a curry for my husband, Bob. As I lifted the lid of my Indian spice box, my senses were heightened. Like an escaping djinn, the fragrances immediately transported me back to India. The only other time I have had this experience was when I visited the small town of Woodford in the Sunshine Coast hinterland, where I grew up. My family moved away, but my grandmother lived there for many years. There were often trips back to see her, and I remember there was one particular bridge over a gully on the outskirts of the town. I would always wind down my window and take in a deep breath, and then…I knew I was home. It was strange how here in India I had this same sense of belonging.

The history of Udaipur fascinated me—from the palaces to the little havelis. Where I was staying at Kankawa, the rooms were built around a central courtyard. My room was reached from the second floor via a steep narrow staircase that hugged the wall, as I did, since there was no handrail. Outside my room, two cane chairs provided a serene view of the lake.

'Get yourself settled and I will come back around midday, and we'll go exploring.' I was so happy to hear Tarun say he would show me around again. We had been in touch during the year, but still I wondered if there would be that same connection between us as there was on my first visit. I had missed him and his family.

Before going to India, I can't say I was a true believer in destiny, but India was to teach me differently. In fact, an astrologer in Udaipur would tell me many years later while reading my palm, that there was a faint, almost invisible line running parallel to my life line, and he believed it was that of Tarun. Was it possible that the story of our friendship had been written long before we had even met?

And yet, on this, my second trip to India, all I knew was that I had a rapport with this man. It wasn't a romantic connection, but a true bond of friendship. I had no way of knowing of the magnitude of the journey that destiny held in store for us or that eventually, he would become my brother and I would become a part of his family, or that our lives would follow those consonant lines for many years. In later times, I found myself examining my palm just to make sure that his line had not disappeared. But all that was ahead of me, all that was unknown. And at this moment, I was simply excited to be back in Udaipur.

Just after noon, Tarun came back to Kankawa to collect me. We walked to the street but I couldn't see his van.

'Where did you park?'

'Here,' he said, pointing to his motorbike. 'You don't mind, do you?'

'Of course not,' I heard myself reply. What was I saying? Was there a helmet in sight? Of course, not.

It took me a moment to remember that I was in a land of 'no rules'. Back home, you must wear a helmet, ride on a particular side of the road, and obey because it is law. Here, I needed to take my own calculated risks, beginning with basics such as the water I drank, the food I ate, the new friends I made and the trust I had in them.

'I'll hold the bike while you get on.'

I stepped onto the sidebar and nonchalantly tried to throw my leg over the other side, steadying myself by holding onto his shoulders. The first attempt failed, but finally I landed on the seat. What an effort! I wasn't quite as flexible as I used to be, that was for sure.

'Ready?'

'Yes!' I gripped his waist and hoped he couldn't feel my sweaty hands through his shirt.

'We'll go to the shop first.'

My experience on motorbikes was limited. I have to admit, there was a sense of freedom mixed with a little recklessness, for the middle-aged North-shore mum, whose normal morning activity might be meeting a friend for a coffee or 'syrup chai' in the newly-expanded shopping expanse of Chatswood Chase. So, with the wind in my hair and sunnies to stop the dust clogging my eyes, my stomach twisted as the bike leapt forward.

It wasn't far to his shop, but there were heaps of, just everything you can imagine, on the road: motorbikes, scooters, tuktuks, pedestrians and even donkeys. I held on tightly. Was it too tight? What was the socially acceptable measure of tightness in this part of the world? I did not wish to overstep the bounds of friendship and offend my friend. Then, I noticed an Indian woman sitting side-saddle behind her husband, not holding on at all. Embarrassed, I released my Tarzan-like grip until we flew around a corner, and I had a close encounter with the arse of a cow that had stopped in the middle of the road, and instinctively grabbed onto him tightly again.

'You okay back there?' he laughed, sensing my fear.

'Fine,' I lied. He turned around to see my face and laughed even more.

'Please don't drop your bundle now, my girl,' I murmured to the cow, thinking I had seen prettier sights as she lifted her tail within inches of my face. Luckily it was to flick a fly.

Other than that, I started to feel quite safe on the back of Tarun's motorbike. Even though it seemed there were no road rules, everyone appeared to know what they were doing. There was certainly no room for hesitation or distraction. A nod or eye contact acted as a 'give way' sign. No words were spoken. Trust was the word of the day. I marvelled at how Indians seemed to have an incredible sense of space, down to the last centimetre.

Whoops, we were off again. There was much honking and beeping of horns on the narrow streets, not meant for so much traffic. The pedestrians had nerves of steel, and sauntered casually amongst the chaos. Suddenly with no forewarning, five donkeys, strung together with ropes, made a dash down the centre of the street and brought the traffic to an abrupt halt. Their backs were laden with building rubble, and a barefoot young woman in a golden yellow sari ran after them, her bangles jingling.

I was suddenly aware of the close proximity of the vehicles around us. My legs almost touched those of the passenger on the scooter beside me—a serious looking man with a thick, black beard and moustache, whose deep, dark, penetrating eyes invaded my personal space. Then I realised, in India, personal space is at a premium and I needed to get used to that as well. His eyes clinched mine; or was he just staring at my blonde hair? I smiled, an offering of friendliness, then reached behind, checking my backpack, suddenly feeling vulnerable.

To my left, a young man pushing a heavily-laden cart came to a standstill beside me, and the smell of freshly-cut herbs and vegetables tickled my nose.

'Namaste,' he smiled.

'Namaste.'

I was relieved to discover a friendly face. Beyond him, a middle-aged foreign woman in a tuktuk was tut-tutting to her travelling companion, as they looked me up and down with eyebrows raised. I immediately loosened my grip on poor Tarun. His beautifully-pressed shirt was now looking decidedly creased. The donkeys passed and the traffic moved on. Food stalls lined our path, and the aromas of chapattis and masala drifted by, interrupted by the smell of manure and bovine urine, running in streams downhill. Children played in the doorways of houses and waved happily as we passed. It was hot and as we gathered speed, the breeze was welcome.

Just as I was getting comfortable, we arrived at Tarun's shop. Heads popped out of neighbouring stores to see who Tarun had on the back of his bike. I saw his friend Naresh from the leather bookshop, and waved.

'Hello, Barbie.' I was touched he remembered my name. The year before I had bought books from him and drank chai at his shop. We parked on the doorstep of Tarun's shop. Until recently, it had been more of an essential oil shop, where huge crystal perfume bottles with decorative stoppers stored sandalwood, rose, geranium and jasmine—pure oils the colour of dark honey, their fragrance intoxicatingly powerful. These containers now lined the upper shelves, and silver jewellery had become the major part of his business. The shop was small, with just one step leading onto the road. The door was kept closed to keep out the dust and noise, as well as the heat.

'What do you think?' he gestured to the glass shelves sparkling with silver, knowing that I was in my element.

'Perfect. Just perfect.'

'Tell me about this wedding you are going to. Maybe, you will need to choose some special pieces for the occasion?' Tarun pressed his lips together tightly, and raised his eyebrows, pretending that he was asking a question, but we both knew it was a statement. Again, I had that strange feeling of being completely at home.

'Chai?' he called, as a young boy magically appeared at the door with a tray of steaming milky tea. I nodded. We sipped our drinks over the glass reception counter, with rings and bracelets gleaming from below.

'I've organised a trip to the Monsoon Palace for you,' he mentioned, as I tried on an ornate necklace for the third time. The Monsoon Palace sits high on the mountains, overlooking the city. I had seen its lights at night and the entire edifice seemed to float in the sky.

'A tuktuk driver will take you, and wait to bring you back.'

Not long after, the driver arrived at the shop and Tarun paid him and issued instructions on where I wanted to go. I had spent quite a bit of time travelling around in these three-wheeled, open-air vehicles that sounded like lawnmowers, so was unfazed. However, we had barely lost sight of the shop when he pulled off to the side and asked me to move into another tuktuk with a different driver. Money changed hands and I began to feel uncomfortable.

'Why do I need to change tuktuks?'

'It is very long way up the mountain,' the first driver told me, 'and my engine is very old. Paresh will take you in his new tuktuk.' It sounded like something out of a *Thomas the Tank Engine* book. I must have looked nervous, as Paresh flashed me a big smile.

'I will take care of you ma'am. Don't worry, you will be safe with me, ma'am.'

Although I had seen the Monsoon Palace from my haveli, I had no idea of its distance. We weaved our way through the narrow streets as I tried to get my bearings. Paresh turned his head to check if I was still looking worried. I wanted him to keep his eyes on the road. 'Where you from, ma'am?'

'Australia,' I replied as quickly as I could, so he wouldn't turn around again.

'I like Australia. Yes, Australia very good. You been to India before?'

'Oh yes, many times,' I said, exaggerating a little.

'You like India?'

'Very much. Very nice people.'

Soon, we were travelling out of the city. When we reached the gates at the bottom of the mountain, Paresh got out and paid the entrance fee. Leaning back, I looked up the mountain range and could see the Monsoon Palace high above.

The road gradient steepened, and the motor of the tuktuk changed to a longer, lower buzz. We inched our way up the vertical incline. A tourist bus passed us on the narrow road, and I wondered if that might have been the wiser option, as I breathed in its oily exhaust fumes. We seemed to be barely moving at all. I found myself pressing my foot to the floor on an imaginary accelerator, willing us to go faster.

I tried to relax and take in the magnificent view. Paresh continued with his non-stop commentary and I leaned closer to the cabin to hear him.

'We are climbing over 1100 feet,' he told me. 'It is very steep…very, very steep. You want to stop for photo?'

'No, no! That's fine. I will take photo at the top.' I had my doubts about the engine restarting at all, if we stopped. The trip took a good 15 minutes, and although we were not travelling fast, vehicles on their return trip were rocketing down the mountain past us. I took a deep breath…and another…and another.

'Can you see the city?' He turned around again.

'Yes. Keep your eyes on the road.'

'Don't worry. I have done this many times,' and he turned again and laughed.

Look at the scenery, I told myself.

The palace was built in 1884. I tried to imagine a long line of elephants carting all the materials up the mountain. Along the side of the road, an old stone wall, that would have been built at the same time, provided some sort of safety barrier.

At last we arrived on a plateau below the palace and Paresh pointed me in the direction of a long flight of stairs. The coach, I noticed, had driven all the way up, but the engine of my chariot reeked of burnt oil, and the driver parked under a tree.

'I'll wait for you here. Take your time, ma'am.'

'You won't go without me, will you?'

'Of course not!'

There was a steep ascent before I reached the steps. I looked back to make sure Paresh was not leaving, but he had propped himself up against the trunk of a tree, and looked like he was going to sleep. The afternoon sun was hot and I paced myself, taking deep breaths so I wouldn't arrive at the top in the midst of a busload of tourists, breathless and dripping in perspiration. Actually, that's too nice a word. In India, you don't perspire. You sweat.

As I reached the top, the 360-degree panorama was spectacular. On one side, the skirt of the mountain unfolded from rocky terrain down to the city and lake below. I could see the outline of the stone wall snaking its way to the peak and the winding road up which the tuktuk had struggled. To the north was a mountain range as far as the eye could see. The afternoon light had cast a bluish haze over the rugged terrain, as the sun began to lower in the sky. Keyhole doorways framed the view. I made my way towards the palace. Although it had fallen into a state of disrepair, it retained an ethereal ambience. I wondered to myself if there was some connection in our minds between being high on a mountain peak, seemingly in the heavens, and the feeling of spirituality and peace. As I looked to the north, there was nothing but peak after peak of desolate, rocky mountain ranges that stretched on forever. Being there made me feel somehow closer to the wonder and beauty of nature's creation in its most elemental form.

On the other side of the palace, a huge balcony overlooked what was the old game reserve below. It would have been an open-air reception area, high above the monsoon clouds. Unfortunately, the ancient walls had been graffitied by tourists leaving their names and dates of their visit.

Steep narrow steps wound their way up to what I would have imagined to be bedrooms, with a view over the ranges. Shards of golden light, pixellated with desert dust, cast long shadows on the floor as the sun began to lower.

The other tourists were heading back to the coach, and besides a couple of locals, who could have been guards or guides, there was only me.

It was time to go. Paresh saw me coming and was ready in his seat.

'You like, ma'am?' he said as he started the engine. The smell of burnt oil seemed to have disappeared.

'Beautiful!'

'Ready?'

'Ready.'

'Not take very long to go down, ma'am.'

He turned the tuktuk around so we were pointing down the mountain, and then whoosh. All my tranquil thoughts were left on the mountaintop as we suddenly sped downwards.

'No brakes, ma'am. Good fun!'

Paresh turned to me, gauging my reaction. For God's sake man, look where you are going! I had been on slower roller-coasters.

'Slow down, Paresh!' I could hear the tremor in my voice.

'No worry, ma'am! Good fun!' He was in his element, and I was growing older and greyer by the second. He turned around again. He was enjoying scaring me. I was sure he could hear my heart thumping as the breeze funnelled through his loose white shirt. Tarun, where are you?

Cars drove slowly up the mountain as we flew around corners. I tried to release my grip from the side of my seat. My knuckles were white, while my brake foot felt like it was going into a spasm from pressing down hard on the floor. I could feel the dust from the road caking on my face with nervous perspiration. I reminded myself, yes, it was calm and peaceful up there.

Tarun had said that the driver would drop me back at my haveli, and as we pulled up, Paresh gave me his card in case I needed a driver the following day. You have to be kidding! I have since heard that tuktuks are no longer allowed on that road. One apparently went over the edge. The name of the driver wasn't mentioned.

I climbed the stairs to my room, tired and dishevelled, and suddenly had a feeling of deja vu. When I was a little girl, I remembered coming home from a day's outing and looking down at the dirty skin peeping out from my sandals, and the clean stripes left when I took them off. It was then, and it seemed now, the sign of a good day. Spills of sticky drinks would have caused dirt to gather in my little shoes. It might have been the local agricultural show, the circus, or maybe a picnic. A bath would have been on the agenda as soon as we got home and that was exactly where I was heading…for a nice, long, hot shower.

The Lake is Full, 2006

Early the next morning, I had trouble tearing myself away from the rooftop. Across the lake was a small pavilion with steps leading to the water, and as I sipped my chai, I watched the busy but unobtrusive activities on the water's edge. On the ghats, I noticed the silhouette of a man practising yoga, his body facing towards the rising sun, while others were having their morning bath. These reflections were mirrored in the lake, and skipped across the static, watery image of the mango trees.

I lifted my gaze to a bird gliding high, its path seemingly crossing the horizon where the Monsoon Palace sat, bathed in pink light as the sun slowly rose. The bird swooped closer, skimmed the lake's surface by the Amet Haveli, and came to rest gracefully on the curved roof of one of its rotundas.

For Christmas, my husband Bob had given me a book called *India* by photographer, Olivier Follmi, further encouraging my interest in India. In its introduction, Radhika Jha quotes an old saying: 'To belong to a place one must know it with the feet.' Although the context to which she was referring was in relation to pilgrimages, I could not help but think of it as I walked the narrow streets of the old city to the spice shop. I passed some of the same people, and they smiled and greeted me with the familiar 'Namaste'.

The first morning, they tried to sell me their wares, but soon realised I was on my way to Spicebox, where Tarun's brother Shakti ran cooking classes and sold Indian spices. It was only a short walk from my haveli. One day, deep in thought, I strode down the lane past the shop, and one of Shakti's neighbours called to me, 'This way,' and pointed me in the right direction. The shops were nothing more than a small room with meagre dwellings above, and I only needed to be momentarily distracted by a colourful piece of fabric flowing in the breeze, or a cow munching on its breakfast, to overstep the entrance to Spicebox.

Everyone was busy sweeping, and preparing to open for business. At one doorway, I saw a tailor already at his antiquated machine, his nimble bare feet in absolute control of the treadle as his fingers guided the blue check cotton. The floor was covered with material and cotton threads. I noticed a sign above the entrance, 'Business Shirts Tailor Made in One Hour'.

A group of schoolgirls laughed and giggled their way past, their spotless white blouses pressed, and long dark hair neatly braided. On the other side an elephant strode towards me, its trunk happily swaying to and fro as if to greet all and sundry. Further on, I found a gallery of miniature paintings in the style of those I had seen with Tarun at the City Palace. The artists were busy applying the finest details with brushes made of only one or two bristles.

A rhythmic tapping drew my attention to a small window, filled to overflowing with shoes of every colour, all sparkling with sequins and beads. The smell of glue and leather permeated the air.

I arrived at the spice shop where the shelves were lined with every conceivable spice and many different Indian teas. Heavy brass pots in all sizes crammed the bottom shelves, and the aromas from Shakti's cooking classes in the adjacent building wafted through the air. Raj, Tarun and Shakti's father, was in attendance, and although speaking no English, pointed to tell me Shakti's whereabouts.

As I stepped back out again, I could see a young boy playfully tapping the rump of a steer as he guided it along the street, and I let him pass before I crossed, dodging the fresh organic message left on the ground by this sacred animal. I climbed the narrow staircase to the kitchen where a cooking class was in progress. I had attended one the previous year. It was a basic classroom with everything being cooked on a single gas burner placed in the centre of a rustic table. A mirror had been placed so that everyone could see both the table and inside the pot as Shakti demonstrated the techniques of Indian cooking. Two American girls were busy shaping potato koftas, placing chopped dried apricot in the centre, while a young man busily chopped ingredients for the next dish. It was hands on, and everyone had a turn. In these days of marble bench tops, double ovens and microwaves, it was refreshing to see how little equipment was required to produce a delicious meal. The most important item, other than the gas burner, was a spice box—a circular metal pot containing the main spices used in Indian cooking.

At the end of the class, the food was eaten and washed down with a Kingfisher beer.

'Hello Barbie,' he smiled as I entered the room. 'This is Barbie. She is from Australia,' he told the class. 'What have you been buying? Show them your earrings.'

I pulled my hair back to reveal the amazing silver, bell-shaped earrings, moving my head so they made a jingly noise, and pointed out the beautiful green emerald stones set above the bell. It was met with such enthusiasm that I needed little encouragement to reveal the turquoise necklace hiding under my blouse, its matching bracelet up my sleeve, and the turquoise and red coral ring on my middle finger. Yes, it had been a very productive time with Tarun in the jewellery shop. At one stage while buying my necklace, I said, 'Hello, Bob!' as I flashed my credit card, knowing the bill would probably arrive home before me.

I worried that I was disrupting Shakti's class, but everyone asked where I had bought such beautiful jewellery. He winked encouragingly, knowing I'd just done an advertisement for their shop. I took a seat as he continued teaching. It looked as if I had arrived just in time for some masala chai. I could smell the cardamom steaming off the hot milk.

It is amazing just how refreshing this drink is even on a hot day. I had taken Shakti's spice mix back to Australia with me, and each cup—made to his specific instructions—had brought back fond memories.

As Shakti served the masala chai to the class, he asked, 'So what are you doing today?'

'Tarun is taking me shopping for clothes for the wedding.'

'Who is getting married?'

'It's the daughter of a family I met in Jaipur.' I checked my watch and realised the time.

'Must go. Tarun will be waiting downstairs.'

And so he was, chatting with his father.

'Are you ready?' he asked. 'Chalo.' Let's go.

We visited several stores, and ended up at one stocking the most exquisite fabrics, the Tulsi Boutique on Bapu Bazar. Tarun spoke to the owner, Mr Rana Krishna, in Hindi, explaining the wedding, and that I wished to have an outfit made. I tried to decide on a fabric. The inevitable sequins and beads sparkled under the fluorescent lights.

'You like chai?' Mr Krishna enquired.

I knew I had just had a cup, but they were small, and anyway, it was bad manners to refuse. He sent the young girl behind the counter to prepare one, and returned to his conversation with Tarun. I wondered just what was transpiring as every now and then, their eyes cast surmising glances in my direction.

'Now! Which colour do you choose, madam?' Mr Krishna enquired.

'I think she should wear yellow,' Tarun was quick to answer before I could get a word in. I was actually quite taken by the deep red. Tarun screwed his face up a little and shook his head. 'How about green? My wife likes green.'

'Turquoise would look good on you,' I heard Mr Krishna chipping in.

'I do like the red.' Anyone listening? It was strange for me to have two men, telling me what colour I should wear.

'When do you need it?' Mr Krishna asked as he took the measurements.

'Tomorrow.' Tarun was quick to answer again.

Hello! Excuse me. I'm over here!

'So, you like yellow?' Mr Krishna pulled the yellow sari from the shelf.

'Okay, let's try yellow, and then can I see the red one?'

There was a full-length mirror and as soon as I wound it around me, it was like I was draped in sunshine. It did look better than I thought.

'Very nice.' Tarun turned his head to one side and the other. 'Yes, very nice.'

'Now can I try the red?'

Mr Krishna held the sequinned fabric up against me.

'It looks beautiful,' said Tarun looking surprised. 'I did not think it would suit you.'

Maybe that is because you are not used to choosing for a blonde, I thought. The sari was six and a half metres and I had brought a sample of the outfit I wanted made.

'I have not made one like this before,' said Mr Krishna, his head moving from side to side as he measured me. 'Are you sure you don't want a traditional button-front shirt?'

I nodded my head.

'Okay!' He said smiling, but at the same time raising his eyebrows at Tarun. 'We will do it.' He let out a long, exasperated breath.

I looked around at the fabrics while he worked out a price.

'So! Now, what shall we do with the yellow?'

Oh, my goodness, give me a break.

'I can make you very nice outfit. Very cheap.' His moustache curled up as he smiled.

'How much?'

It was the equivalent of around $A40. I weakened.

'Okay, okay! Yellow.'

'Very good.' Mr Krishna clapped his hands together, having finally worn me down.

By that stage, they were both smiling, and I couldn't help but laugh.

'It will be ready tomorrow,' he said as we left. I was relieved to be organised for the wedding, and as excited as I was, I was sorry to be leaving Udaipur the next day. I knew it would be at least another 12 months before I returned. Tarun noticed that I was a bit quiet in the car as we drove back to my haveli.

'Family is looking forward to seeing you tonight,' he told me with a big smile. 'Children are excited.'

Just at dusk, Tarun called at Kankawa to take me to the family home. I was getting used to riding on the back of his motorbike. It was particularly refreshing in the cool of the early evening. The dim streetlights dotted along the way did little to help see the bicycles, pedestrians and cows on the road. It amazed me how many rode their bikes at night with no headlights. We stopped along the way to buy some sweets. I had also brought some gifts with me this time.

As we arrived at the house, a neighbour was tending to his elephants that were tethered on the next block. It was strange to see these massive animals in a suburban environment.

'Would you like to take a closer look?' Tarun waved to his neighbour and led me across the road and through the gate to where the elephant stood, towering over the fence that enclosed it.

'She's very tame. You can pat her,' his neighbour offered. 'Here, on her trunk is best.' It was almost dark, but I could see the eyes of the huge creature looking at me and I imagined it thinking— just another human to entertain. I touched her gently on the trunk and felt her leathery skin and the short spikey hairs that grew between her wrinkles.

'Hello girl,' I said as I stroked her. Colourful designs, only just visible in the fading light, had been painted on her forehead, and I noticed one ear was mottled in paler skin.

'She's very old,' he told me. Long eyelashes brushed against my fingers as she slowly blinked.

'I think it's her bedtime,' I told him as I said goodbye. 'Thank you.'

On the other side of the road, the children had rushed out to greet us as soon as they'd heard the motorbike, making me feel most welcome. Tarun's wife Manisha, along with Poonam, Shakti's wife, greeted me at the front door. They made a colourful picture in bright yellow and lime green. I saw where Tarun got his colour choices for me. I was excited to see them again.

'Namaste.' They welcomed me in. They looked so elegant, draped in beautiful silk and immaculately made up with thick black kohl outlining their dark eyes. Each wore a bindi to match their sari. Inside, Mamma was waiting. Wisps of silver hair peeped from beneath the shawl of her red sari, framing her face. She held my hands in hers as we spoke, and directed me to sit beside her. We sat in the front room where two sofas also acted as beds for the children. Raj, Tarun's father, came and greeted me, and then retired back to his room. Rudrakshi climbed onto her father's lap and draped her arms around him.

I had brought my so-called 'holy water' (gin), which had gone down a treat on the last trip. Tarun and I had a gin and tonic. The women, of course, did not drink, but did love the Estee Lauder perfumes I had bought for them.

Soon, the smells of fresh chapattis and potato curry wafted through the house, and were brought to the table with a salad of tomatoes and cucumber. A warm rice pudding followed. We shared the sweets I had collected along the way. Some were set in silver leaf and others were either very pink or vibrant green. Indians love their sweets. Many are made from milk that has been boiled with sugar, ending up like our condensed milk, and then flavoured with carrot, pistachio nuts and spices.

Time passed too quickly. 'Come!' called Tarun. 'I'll take you back.'

The streets were empty; mostly in darkness, and fraught with obstacles. A skinny cat with an unusual flat tail ran out in front of us using up one of its nine lives. There were no streetlights. As we rounded a corner, our headlights projected a silhouette of a cow with huge horns on the unlit wall of an old building. All security shutters were down, and except for a few mangy dogs wandering around scavenging the rubbish heaps, the city had gone to sleep.

Once back at Kankawa, I noticed the heavy timber front door was closed. It was late. Tarun came to the door with me and gave it a push. It opened. I was nervous, as Bambi, the German Shepherd, was on security. She had given me a good sniff on my arrival a few days ago, and I was hoping that she remembered me. I had heard her give one guest a noisy welcome the night before. Sure enough, she was waiting inside the door. I have to admit, I am not brave with large dogs, and I froze as she came over to give me the all clear. The night doorman was asleep on a nearby chair and did not stir. Bambi wagged her tail and I made a quick scamper up the stairs, waving goodnight to Tarun as he pulled the door closed, and then, sticking close to the wall, I carefully made my way up the narrow staircase to my room, and heaved a sigh of relief as I closed my door behind me.

Meeting Tarun, 2005

That night, as I got into bed, I smiled to myself as I recalled my first visit and how much I felt at home back in Udaipur. It had not been 12 months since my first trip, and I had no idea then, that I would be back in India so soon. I set my alarm as Tarun was picking me up in the morning, and I then took my diary out of my bag and flipped the pages back to March 2005, when my friend Brigitte invited me to join her on a buying trip for her shop, Namastai. Previously, I'd minded her store in Sydney while she travelled.

We'd flown direct to Mumbai from Sydney and overnighted in the luxury of the Leela Kempinski before our early morning flight to Udaipur.

A shining white limousine had collected us from Mumbai airport amid hundreds of tiny yellow taxicabs and buzzing tuktuks. I could see how some people would find India daunting—maybe too daunting. There is no easy entry, no way of slowly easing oneself into India. Like biting into a raw chilli, my shock was immediate. The air was close. The people were close. Millions of people were close: in fact, 20 million people were close. I found it hard to imagine myself out there, amongst it. It scared me.

'Keep your windows up,' our chauffer had warned as desperate faces pressed against the windows when the traffic came to a halt. Small children, still babies by our standards, dashed in amongst the cars selling newspapers and cigarettes, and skinny mothers holding scrawny babies rushed to the car—a beacon of wealth—like moths to a light.

Ragged, dirty cloth and bits of old, torn plastic held together with bamboo and rope provided shelters along the side of the road. Women and children sat by small open fires preparing food, while grubby little toddlers with matted hair, crawled in the dust within inches of the traffic.

Yet within the bounds of the hotel lay absolute luxury: this was probably the most amazing hotel I had ever stayed at. But then, I could have been anywhere in the world. I knew the real India lay outside those parameters.

The next morning, we were on a 6 am flight to Udaipur, and left the hotel in the same luxury as we had arrived.

'Shakti may come and pick us up at the airport,' Brigitte had told me as the plane touched down in Udaipur. They'd had business dealings on her previous trip and had kept in contact. As we walked out of the terminal, he was there with his younger brother, Tarun. That was the day Tarun and I first met. He was the taller of the two, and his gentle smile extended the same welcome as his brother Shakti. Once the introductions were complete, our luggage was packed into the back of their transit van, and with Brigitte and I in the back seat, they drove us to the hotel that Shakti had reserved, the recently-opened Udai Koti.

That morning as we drove towards Udaipur, I felt more relaxed and less conspicuous in the modest van, than in Mumbai in the limousine. Cheery faces smiled and waved as they passed. I felt welcomed. Although there was still a lot of traffic, nobody seemed to be in a rush. Lorries were delivering their goods to town—big old-fashioned trucks laden to the hilt with loads often twice as wide as the vehicle, while haphazardly covered in ragged hessian and secured by a web of rope and knots. Their cabins were painted and decorated in the brightest of colours, with garlands and streamers flying in the breeze, and the dashboards covered in statues of the Gods Lakshmi, Ganesh and Krishna to protect them on the road.

All around was the constant beeping of horns. In the rear-vision mirror, dark sunglasses hid Tarun's eyes as he drove confidently in silence. Horns honked as cyclists on antiquated bicycles tried their best to avoid the potholes on the uneven edge of the rough bitumen. Cows wandered here and there, oblivious to any danger, and seemed to know their majestic place, sometimes sitting in the middle of the dusty road as traffic diverted around them.

Sparkling mirror mosaics caught the morning light at the entrance to Udai Koti. A barefoot boy was busy sweeping the black and white chequered floors with a straw brush.

'Namaste,' he greeted us with bowed head and hands in prayer position.

'Namaste,' replied Shakti.

'They will let us know when your room is ready. Come. We'll have breakfast while we wait.' Shakti directed us up the staircase to the roof terrace. Conversations in French, German and Japanese blurred into each other as we made our way to a table overlooking the parched lake. After having seen so many brochures capturing the beauty of the lake, I was devastated to see it empty. The country was in drought. Cattle had found their way to new grazing ground as grass sprouted on the lakebed. All that remained were a few puddles. Grounded in one of these was a large red and blue boat.

'That's the boat from *Octopussy*,' I pointed out to Brigitte.

'You know that movie?' Tarun asked.

'They're all James Bond fans at my house,' I laughed.

Tarun's face lit up. 'I remember when they came to Udaipur to film it, I was just a young boy. It was so exciting.' And for a moment, I caught a glimpse of that young boy as he looked out towards the boat. There was something gentle in his manner that impressed me.

In the movie, there had been tuktuk chases down the narrow streets, scenes at the Palace, and yes, James Bond being rowed across the lake in that magical boat by scantily clad, beautiful women.

'There is a restaurant by the lake that has played that movie every night since then,' he added. 'It was a proud moment for our city.'

The waiter appeared at our table. 'You like masala chai?'

'You mean tea?' The popularity of chai had not yet reached Australia.

'Chai is tea, but masala chai is tea with spices; cardamom, cinnamon—many spices. Very nice. Very, very nice.'

'Yes, please,' Brigitte and I nodded in unison.

I recall being amazed as I watched Tarun and Shakti load their chai with spoonful after spoonful of sugar.

'Indians drink their tea very sweet,' he smiled, catching me out of the corner of his eye.

'How are Poonam and the children?' Brigitte asked Shakti. I had seen the family photos from her last visit and was looking forward to meeting them.

'They're all very good.' His head waggled from left to right as he spoke. 'They're looking forward to seeing you. The children are speaking some English now.'

'You have shop too?' Tarun asked me as we sipped our chai.

'No, Barbie's an artist,' Brigitte replied.

'My uncle's a famous Indian artist,' he seemed pleased to add. 'You must meet him when you go to Jaipur.'

After breakfast, they helped take our luggage to the room. At each landing were bowls of floating flowers, bright orange and gold marigolds, arranged in floral motifs with sweet smelling jasmine blossoms. Incense wafted through the air. It was the India I had imagined. Our room was light and spacious, and Shakti and Tarun took a seat by the window and ate the complimentary biscuits while we organised our belongings.

'As the lake is dry, we can walk across to our shop. Much shorter. We'll show you the way,' Shakti said as we walked back down the stairs. We made our way down the street by the Amet Haveli, a heritage-listed building that was in the process of renovation, carefully stepping around two cows that had decided to sit in the middle of the narrow lane. Tarun walked ahead with his brother. I wondered if he might be a little shy. Brigitte and I followed along behind. Shakti stopped and spoke to a man in the garden and then signalled us to come as well.

'That was Mr Singh. He owns this place. He said it is okay to show you around. Next time you come, it will be finished.'

A solid, old timber door led to a room of cool, rendered white walls and beyond, we could see the vista across the lake to the city through a series of arched windows. A carved wooden seat, heavily laden with cushions hung on chains from the ceiling. I have since seen it written up in a book by Alastair Sawday called *Special Places to Stay in India*. He wrote:'The luxury lies not in opulent furnishings or obsequious staff, but in that feeling that you have found somewhere genuinely special.'

I could only imagine how it would be to stay there when the lake was full.

'We'll eat here tonight at the restaurant.' Shakti pointed to the tables and chairs under a huge mango tree. 'Come. Let's walk across to the palace.' We walked across the rocky path to the Lake Palace, now in dry-dock. A four-wheel drive zoomed past, kicking up the dust as it ferried guests to the palace. A red carpet lay down the full length of the stairs, but there was a huge drop down from the last step, which would normally have been the water's edge. The palace was indeed baring her bones, as dried-out black weed clung to the walls below the watermark. An elephant, dwarfed by this gracious old building stood to attention by the stairs, its face decorated in painted motifs and its ankles encrusted in sparkling red sashes. A young man snoozed on his back.

We wandered around the perimeter of the palace, our heads well below the dirty water line that stained the whitewashed walls, and then across to the other side of the lake and up the steep stairs of Gangaur Ghat, leading to the old part of the city.

'Normally, this would be where the women would do their washing and bathe,' Tarun told us. 'Now, they gather at the wells.' So much of everyday life was affected by the drought.

It was there that we bade our farewells.

'I have organised some appointments for you. I'll pick you up after lunch,' Shakti told Brigitte.

And with that, the quiet Tarun announced, 'I'll be your guide this afternoon, Barbie. Don't go anywhere without me. I'll pick you up after lunch, and we will go to the City Palace. See you at 1:00 pm.'

So there it was, I had a guide. I knew I would feel comfortable and safe with him. I had an unexplainable feeling of trust in this man I had met only hours before.

Later, when I met him downstairs at reception, he had changed into jeans and a Levi Strauss T-shirt and looked much more relaxed. He was a handsome young man whose quiet manner put me at ease.

From my haveli, we drove across to the other side of the lake and found a park within walking distance of the entrance to the palace. The narrow, cobbled streets were lined with market stalls selling all kinds of wares. Faded samples of traditional Indian kurtas hung outside in the sun, collecting dust.

'Come inside, ma'am. We have more inside. Many colours, ma'am. Many styles.'

'Beautiful silver jewellery, ma'am,' a voice called from the other side of the road. Near him, an old man sat on a hessian bag, chipping away at a piece of marble. He looked up and gave me a smile and pointed to his creations, laid out in front of him.

'You like buy ma'am. Very cheap.'

'I'll come back later,' I promised. I hadn't wanted to carry marble around on my tour of the palace.

'There are many marble quarries near Udaipur,' Tarun explained as we walked. 'The street carvers collect the small offcuts and do their sculptures from them. Nothing is wasted.'

I sidestepped a fresh cow pat, and was startled by the toot of a motorbike as it sped by dangerously close. Tarun put out a protective arm and shot the rider an angry glare. It would take me some time before I could walk confidently in the streets, and not worry about being hit by a motorbike.

We arrived at the entrance to the palace, known as Hati Pol. Two imposing gates with huge protruding spikes had, in the past, protected the palace, should the enemy charge on elephants.

'Since you are an artist, I think we should start with the art gallery,' Tarun said as he led me up some narrow stairs. 'Our history has been recorded in these paintings.' He pointed out artworks depicting huge battles, as well as processions and celebrations. Beside them hung suits of armour, swords and many other types of weapons. Although it was stifling hot outside, the thick walls created a cool sanctuary from the afternoon sun.

We trailed along behind a tour being given by one of the palace guides. Mosaics of peacocks, symbolic of Rajasthan, decorated the walls, while red and blue-stained windows cast colourful patterns on the floor.

We followed the tour into the main bedroom, when someone asked, 'How come there is not a bed in here?'

The guide's answer made everyone chuckle. 'With *Kama Sutra*, there is no need for a bed.' Eyes rolled. Tarun said nothing, and I did not make eye contact. It was not the conversation I wanted to have with a man I had just met. 'The Maharaja had over 1500 wives.' Everybody gasped. The walls and ceilings of the dome-shaped bedroom were covered in mirrors that romantically reflected the light of candles and lamps. Through the windows, I was able to see the Lake Palace, on the dry lake where cattle grazed.

'It must be beautiful when it's full,' I commented as we paused for the view.

'Very beautiful. Did you know, the Palace on the Lake was built by Maharana Jagat Singh as a present for his wife?'

'Really.' What an amazing present.

From the other side, I had been able to get a good view of the city below. Washing hung from the windows and on the rooftops of the multicoloured buildings—blue, turquoise, yellow and dusty white—old buildings that had been continually added to, fighting each other for a view of the lake.

'So, what do you think of India so far?' asked Tarun.

'I like it—especially Udaipur.'

'Tell me about your family. Are you married? Do you have children?'

'Yes, I am married. My husband is Bob. We've been married for 30 years now. He's a lovely man. You'd like him. He is tall, even taller than you—6 feet 5 inches.'

'Goodness!'

'Yes, and we have two sons, Chris is 24 and Tim is 22. You?'

'My wife is Manisha, and my daughter Rudrakshi, she is six. You must come to my house for dinner. You'll meet them.'

The time passed quickly. I learnt a lot about Indian culture and history that afternoon, and made a new friend as well. He was very easy to talk to and I'd enjoyed his company.

'We'll go to the shop,' he said when we arrived back at the van. 'Brigitte should also be there by now. Would you like to see some jewellery?' He raised his eyebrows and tilted his head to one side in a knowing way.

'Yes, of course.' What a silly question.

'I'll take you to a friend's shop. He'll give you good price.'

We collected Brigitte along the way. The traffic was chaotic. 'I won't come in. There's no parking. Tell my friend to call me when you are finished and I'll come back.'

The dusty exterior and faded cloth in the window gave no indication of what we would find inside.

'We could be a while in here,' Brigitte said as our eyes raced around the room at shelves brimming with silver jewellery. The shopkeeper carefully weighed each piece, and then used his calculator to determine the price. Once given the nod, they were placed in cloth bags. We were both more than happy with our stash of treasures.

'Come back again,' he called, waving goodbye as we climbed back into Tarun's van. By that stage, it was getting dark outside. Brigitte wanted to buy diaries for her shop, so we dropped her off at Naresh's leather shop. We'd been on the go all day. I slumped back in my seat, glad to be off my feet. Tarun was quick to notice.

'You look bored.' I wasn't. I was probably just daydreaming about all that had happened in what was still my first day in Udaipur, and really my first full day in India.

'Come, I'll take you to the Sunset Gardens,' and with that we were away again. The gardens were on a hill overlooking the palace on the lake, which was now lit up. When not in drought, a water fountain played music every evening. Even without the music it was a lovely vantage point, and a refreshingly cool place to take a walk in the evening air.

'What would you like to do tomorrow? I'm free. There are temples not too far from here. I can take you.'

'Are you sure you don't have other things you need to do?'

He insisted and so it was planned. By the time we got back, Brigitte had completed her business dealings. We had a quick freshen up at the hotel before walking down to dinner. The Ambrai restaurant took on a different appearance at night as lights were strung from the branches of the mango trees. Lit up like the Queen Mary, the Lake Palace could very well have been surrounded by water, as darkness hid the dusty lakebed.

We were given a table with the best view, thanks I am sure, to the friendship between the owners and Shakti. A young man sat on a rug on the ground and played gentle music on his sitar. The stars shone brightly in the sky, illuminated further by a glorious moon.

We were happy to let the boys suggest courses from the menu and dined on tandoori potatoes, dal, roti, naan and a mixed vegetable dish. It was most delicious. Ambrai has since become my favourite restaurant.

'What are you doing tomorrow?' Brigitte asked me as we finished off.

Before I could say anything, Tarun piped in, 'I'm taking her to the temples. Now, it's getting late. We must go home to our wives. See you tomorrow.'

It had been a long day since our early departure from Mumbai and Brigitte and I were asleep in no time. Around

4 am, I was shaken from the depths of sleep by the early morning call to prayer from the minaret of the nearby mosque. Brigitte slept on regardless. I lay awake for a while thinking about my first day. I already knew that I would be returning to this place. India was different from anywhere else I had ever been. The colours of every aspect were amazing and inspired the artist in me.

My mind was active, and there was no way I was going back to sleep. By 6:30 am, I had gone to the rooftop. I sat, mesmerised by the sunrise, as the haze lifted from the bordering mountains. The rose pink of the sky changed to mauve and then blue. I ordered masala chai and wondered if I could possibly capture the moment in a painting when I got home. I wrote and sketched in my diary.

Later in the day, I began my excursion to the temples with Tarun. It was indeed an experience I won't forget. The first roundabout we came to took a marathon effort to execute. I had never seen such chaos. As I sat in the front seat of the transit van, my window down, I didn't dare put my elbow on the window edge in case I knocked the person beside me off his bicycle; it was that close. There were no lights, no traffic officer, just hundreds of people in all manners of transport—cars, motorbikes, tuktuks, camels, pushbikes—all converging on the same roundabout, as a 'sacred' cow lay in the middle of it all, completely unfazed by the tooting of horns and motorbikes buzzing by.

I was relieved when we were finally on our way again, but turned my head to make sure the woman balancing a huge terracotta pot on her head had made it safely to the other side of the road.

The temples were up in the mountains behind Udaipur, and the roads were winding and narrow, and not in the best of repair. Many people travel to work in the city each day by bus or lorry. The buses were crowded, with people spilling onto the rooftop, their legs dangling over the edge. We passed an old lorry that had failed to make the trip, abandoned and rusting on the side of the road. People were now living in it. There were no safety barriers, only a few strategically-placed boulders between the edge and the steep drop over the side.

Cars and motorbikes or scooters were expected to overtake the buses and lorries, and toot their horns with little distance between them and the oncoming traffic. In fact, most vehicles had a sign 'Horn Please' painted on the rear, and at every passing, the horns let out weird musical tunes. This did not slow down the traffic as trucks and buses headed directly for each other on the wrong side of the road, veering only at the last minute to avoid a collision. My heart was in my mouth.

'I don't usually swear,' I told Tarun, 'but you may learn a few new words today.' A bus had been heading towards us on the wrong side of the road. I grabbed the edge of my seat. Its horn rang out as we sought safety on the gravel edge of the road.

'Don't worry,' he laughed. 'This is India!'

Our first stop was a village called Kailashpura, about half an hour out of the city. As we drove down the steep road into the village, we slowed down as a woman guided her herd of goats back home. On her head, a high stack of firewood; behind her, the turquoise scarf of her sari trailed in the breeze like a kite. As we pulled to the side of the road opposite the temple, I noticed a group of men standing in a circle a few feet down.

'What are they doing?' I naively asked.

Tarun hesitated, and then couldn't contain his laughter. 'It's a urinal.'

How embarrassing. How extremely embarrassing. My hand automatically covered my mouth and felt the warmth in my face as it undoubtedly turned a rosy red. Once I opened the door to get out, the odour hit me—yes, that was definitely a urinal. I wanted to hold my nose, but instead tried momentarily not to breathe. If I were to list the ten most embarrassing moments in my life, that would be high on the list.

'Come this way,' he said trying to hide his amusement as he led me into a small shop. 'We will leave our shoes here.' Sandalwood oil burned in the corner and I took a deep breath to clear my head of my 'faux pas' as well as the lingering smell.

As we walked outside, a tourist bus pulled up and passengers were making their way into the main entrance hall of the temple. The floor was strewn with hundreds of shoes of every size and colour, and I then realised why Tarun had chosen to leave ours back there with the storekeeper.

'But I don't want to take my shoes off,' I heard the shriek of a loud American woman. 'Why do I have to take my shoes off?'

I cringed. There is a quote by James Michener, 'If you reject the food, ignore the customs, fear the religion and avoid the people, you might better stay at home.' That may have been her better option.

I had done some research on the temples the previous night. Known as Eklingji, and surrounded by high walls, the temple complex comprised of some 108 small temples carved in marble and granite, and was built over a water spring. It was a revered place of devotion for Hindu pilgrims in India, and dated back to 971 AD.

'This is one of the most famous temples of Rajasthan,' Tarun explained. 'There are two tanks built over the water spring, and water from these tanks is consumed during services of the Lord.'

On climbing the steps to the entrance, we came across the queue of tourists lined up outside the roped-off area, waiting to view the deities. The floor was abundant with offerings of fruit, and women and children sat cross-legged threading flowers into garlands. Incense wafted through the air. The worn marble floor felt tantalisingly cool and smooth under my feet as I followed my friend past the tourists.

'Come through here,' Tarun lifted the rope, beckoning me to follow.

'Are you sure?' I asked, looking behind me, not wanting to do the wrong thing.

'It's okay. I am going to pray. Rope is for tourists.'

'Why is SHE going under the rope?' Oh no. I heard the embarrassing twang of the now barefoot American.

'Come on,' he said quietly. We both giggled, trying not to laugh out loud. I probably should have thanked her. It was the first of many laughs we shared that day.

The ambience of the temples was intoxicating. We sat in silence near one of the smaller temples, breathing in the faint fragrances of incense and the floral tributes. I closed my eyes and felt the weight of my shoulders drop. I thought of the many people in whose footsteps I had trod, and how each bare foot had, over centuries, worn down the marble floor.

'Should we go? 'Tarun stood up.

We wandered back towards the entrance, collected our shoes, and were soon on our way again. The road ahead was even steeper, as we drove into the high mountainous areas, where the drought had taken its toll on the vegetation.

We passed people walking their animals—seemingly in the middle of nowhere, more than likely looking for water—and then came across shanty type shelters strung between the trees. These structures were more often than not, a ragged piece of dusty blue canvas or plastic sheeting.

The next stop, the Sas-Bahu Temple, was in a remote area, this one partially in ruins. Intricate sculpture, depicting scenes from the *Kama Sutra* covered every pillar. It was not immediately obvious, and it was only after I had stood intently peering at a sculpture and stepped back, that

I realised that these were erotic Indian love-making scenes. I felt another flush of heat on my cheeks.

'Too many pieces have been removed—stolen—and sold off to collectors in different parts of the world. There is security now,' Tarun explained. I noticed broken pillars and denuded spaces where whole sculptures had been taken. 'It is sad that some men spent their whole life working on these temples,' he added, 'and others deem it their right to pillage our history.' The complexity of the carvings was incredible.

We took a seat on the steps and had the cool drinks we had bought along the way. Three Indian men were standing over in the corner having a cigarette. They spoke and gestured to Tarun in Hindi, and at the same time looked me up and down. He looked down at his drink, twirling it in his hands. I could tell he was not comfortable with something they had said. He shook his head and did not answer them.

'Do you know them?' I asked.

'No,' he replied and shook his head again.

'What's wrong?'

'They think we are "together" and made some remarks.' I waited for him to continue. 'Some people cannot understand that an Indian man and a tourist woman can be friends. They have small minds.' I could tell he was embarrassed, more for me than for himself. The men continued to stare.

'Well, I'm glad I have you as my friend,' I told him. He smiled.

'Chalo. Let's go.'

We walked back to the van, and headed back along the winding road to Udaipur. By that time of day, the heavily-laden buses were making their way back up the mountainside, bringing home workers from the city. The passengers smiled and waved from the rooftop as we passed, holding on precariously with the other hand. A couple of hundred metres up the road, a heavy truck had broken down right on a sharp curve. I braced myself as a brightly-painted truck tooted its musical horn and sped directly towards us, only to move to the other side at the last minute. What seemed like a swarm of scooters and motorbikes buzzed their way home—no helmets of course, and with three, sometimes four people on board all lined up with the precision of sardines in a can.

By the time we got back to the city, the traffic was absolutely chaotic, coming to a standstill leading up to the bridge across the lake, and my haveli.

'Drop me off on this side and I can walk across the lake,' I told him.

He didn't look convinced. 'Are you sure? The lake is full of beggars at this time of night.'

'I'll be fine.'

He parked his van on the edge of the barren lake, and if it wasn't for the stairs, I'm sure he would have driven me across. I could feel two eyes burning into my back until I reached the safety of the steps by the Amet Haveli. Women collected the pats left by the grazing cattle. An emaciated young mother had placed herself directly in my path whilst holding her equally gaunt, crying baby. She gestured with her hands to her mouth and then to the whimpering lips of the tiny infant wrapped in a dirty cloth. She swished her hand to remove a fly that circled the baby's infected eye. I felt a lump in my throat and gave her the ten rupee note I already had in my hand. She smiled and moved on to the next person. I turned as I reached the other side, and Tarun was still there. I waved. He flicked his headlights in answer.

As I walked back up the winding road, the soft glow of the low voltage street lights led the way, and the Ambrai restaurant was beginning to serve dinner under the setting sun. Normally the view would have been over the lake and the reflections of the palace, but tonight the view at dusk was of the beggars and the cattle, and as the light faded, so did their images. I wondered if the little children went home or if they were still running around in the dark. I wanted to think that they were all tucked up in their beds but only the night would know.

Jaipur, 2005

Every day was an adventure on that first trip to Udaipur. We only spent a week there, but I felt, I got to know Tarun. Brigitte and I were invited to the family home for dinner on our last night.

'My wife wants to meet you,' Tarun told me as we drove out to the house. 'Everyday, I say, "Barbie and I went to the Palace; Barbie and I went to the temples; Barbie and I went to the Ambrai."' His face dropped.

'Today, she said to me, "I want to meet this Barbie!"' He gave me a most serious look, and then seeing my face, burst into laughter. 'Don't worry, I was just teasing.'

I shook my finger at him. 'You had me worried.'

On our arrival, his daughter Rudrakshi greeted us at the gate with a big smile and a huge hug for her father. She was definitely Daddy's girl. Following close behind were Shakti's two children, Riya and Mahipal. Rudrakshi grabbed her father's hand and led us into the front room where his mother, introduced as Mamma, was sitting. 'She doesn't speak any English,' Tarun mentioned, as she gestured me to the seat beside her. She took my hand and I immediately felt warmth towards her. Her hands were tiny and she wore several rings on her fingers, a gold anklet and ring on her toe. Her nails were painted a soft shade of pink. She wore a pink sari, and her hair hung in a long plait down her back. She was a sweetie—I could tell.

Spicy aromas drifted in from the kitchen. Tarun disappeared out of the room and reappeared with his wife Manisha and Poonam, Shakti's wife. Behind him was his father Raj, a tall man with huge dark, gentle eyes. Manisha was in pink, and Poonam in orange, their eyes highlighted in kohl. Sparkling bindis decorated their foreheads. They were both beautiful young women, and although speaking very little English, greeted us enthusiastically.

Tarun spoke to them in Hindi, and then translated. I could hear my name spoken. 'I told them you have two sons. Show them their photos.' Mamma pointed to the photo of Bob. 'My husband,' I told her. Mamma nodded her head and smiled, and then pointed to me. I put my hand on my heart and nodded back. 'Ahh,' she said.

Manisha placed some snacks on the low table and Tarun brought a bottle of chilled Kingfisher beer from the fridge and poured a glass each for Brigitte and I, plus one for himself.

'Shakti will be back when he finishes his cooking class,' he said as he sipped on his drink. Sometimes he taught two classes a day, the evening one finishing around 8 pm. Manisha and Poonam returned to the kitchen. The children jumped about as children all over the world do, excited to have visitors. It was a happy household.

When Shakti arrived, we moved to the dining table and Manisha and Poonam began to serve dinner. Tarun brought a chair for Mamma, who sat at the end, the gentle matriarch of the family. She had eaten earlier. Dinner was a delicious mixture of tomato salad, spicy potatoes and a continual supply of hot chapattis.

Indians seem to eat quite late, so once dinner was over, Tarun indicated that it was time to go, and we bade our farewells.

'I'll pick you up in the morning at eight to go to the airport,' he told us on the way back. We were leaving for Jaipur the next day.

'You have a lovely family. I'm sad to be leaving,' I told him.

'We will miss you,' he replied. 'Text me from Jaipur.'

Bob had been waiting to hear about a job offer in Singapore and early the next morning he phoned to tell me the job had been confirmed, and we would be moving within a few weeks of my arrival back in Sydney. There was a lot going on in my head. There I was on my first trip to Asia, and then suddenly, I was about to move to that side of the world. I felt a shiver of excitement.

Brigitte and I flew on to Jaipur and I spent my first of many stays at the Diggi Palace. It is a popular place with tourists from all over the world, and is also well known for hosting the annual Jaipur Literature Festival.

Once checked in, we were directed to the rooftop restaurant while our rooms were made ready. A barefoot old man in a well-worn dhoti and turban tended an open fire, as he cooked breakfast for the guests. The once white walls of the old building bore the weary signs of years of exposure to the elements. Tortured bougainvillea hung from the window boxes.

From our table, we could see peacocks wandering freely in the garden below, occasionally flaunting their full plumage. Green parrots fluttered on the edge of the birdbath. It was a tranquil refuge from the rush of the city.

At the table next to us were seated an Indian man and a European. As I looked at the European, I noticed his baggy white Indian pants and shirt, that he had unfashionably combined with a blue baseball hat. Long curly hair fell from under the cap. The Indian man however was dressed in western clothing.

As we ordered some food, the European asked with an obvious French accent, 'And what brings you girls to Jaipur?'

'I'm on a buying trip for my business. Are you French?' Brigitte was quick to ask.

'Oui. And you?'

That led to an enthusiastic exchange in French, with him sharing where he bought his products in Jaipur.

Wilson, the hotel manager, appeared at the table. 'Your room is ready ma'am,' and he gave me the keys. 'The best room in the palace.' Actually, I wouldn't call it a palace, but more like a gracious old residence.

I thought back to Udaipur. I missed the quaintness of the old city. In Jaipur, the roads were wider and busier, with so many more people. It had been kind of Tarun to take us to the airport that morning. 'I'll text you,' he had called out as he dropped us off.

In the meantime, the Frenchman had given Brigitte his card and that of the Indian man, Sharma, his quality supervisor. 'You need someone here to check your goods before they are sent,' he told her. 'Sharma does this for me. Returning faulty goods to India is not an option. It's far too expensive.'

Sadly, that afternoon, Brigitte received word from her supplier, who she had especially come to see, that they could no longer fulfil her order. Someone else from Australia had placed a larger order and demanded exclusivity. Loyalty goes to the highest bidder. That's business in India.

She was rather down, and so we decided to go shoe shopping, and called Sharma to see if he could recommend anywhere. Surprisingly, he arrived within minutes on his scooter. His wife had just had a baby a couple of days prior, and we were not expecting him to turn up.

'Don't worry about it tonight,' Brigitte insisted. 'Go home to your wife.'

'My mother is with her,' he said. 'Baby is crying. Crying all the time. Tonight suits me.' He smiled and called a taxi.

The shoe store was jam-packed; shoes reaching up some four metres to the ceiling, with rustic wobbly ladders for access. A narrow set of stairs led to the basement and even more shoes. I was busy upstairs when I was startled by a scream from Brigitte, echoing from the dark depths below, followed by a hurried exit up the stairs, much to the amusement of Sharma, the owner and his two sons.

'Rats!' Brigitte mouthed to me as she tried to compose herself. 'HUGE rats!'

Once she managed to calm herself, she got back to the serious business of shoe buying. She tried the shoes on in her size to gauge the fit and quality, with the owner seated at her feet, smiling every time she bent over to fit a shoe. I could hear comments.

'Nice!'

'Oh yes, very nice.'

'Beautiful!' I turned to see all three seated at her feet, getting a 'very nice' view of her cleavage each time she bent down! I signalled to her and she took a more upright position. Shoes were ordered.

'I hope you got a good price after all that,' I said as we laughed all the way back to our 'palace'.

Early next morning, we called a driver, Omesh whom Brigitte had employed on her previous visit. He drove us out of the city to the factory that the Frenchman had suggested. Costs of drivers are cheap in India, and it was more economical for us to pay him to wait the two to three hours than to order another taxi when we were finished.

The factory was just what Brigitte needed and the people running it were very welcoming. They had turned what was virtual desert into a beautiful place by planting hundreds of trees, and employed local men and women, and taught them the art of sewing, beading, pattern making etc.

The respect shown to the workers was evident, unlike some of the oppressive, dingy factories we had previously visited. Anu, the owner, offered to help Brigitte with her production.

We were invited to join her and her husband Rohit, along with their farm managers for a tasty vegetarian lunch made with produce from the garden. Later, while Brigitte chose garments, Rohit showed me over the property. Arrangements were made for me to come back the following day to collect some samples.

'Come back for lunch again tomorrow,' Anu called to me as we left.

Next morning, Brigitte had some work to do, so organised for me to go and see the Amer Fort. Unfortunately, Omesh, her driver, had double booked and sent another driver. He seemed nice enough, but made me feel nervous when he began issuing instructions.

'If anyone stops us, you must say that we are friends, not that I am your driver,' he told me after Omesh left. 'I'll take you to the Fort and wait for you.'

I wished Tarun were there. He would be able to tell me how to handle the situation. I climbed into the front seat, as there were no seatbelts in the back. My driver informed me that he had just picked up his car that morning. He was so proud. It was brand new; so much so that it still had the plastic covering on the upholstery. I knew because I was sticking to it, and wondered if he had just picked up his licence as well.

'You are my first customer,' he told me proudly. I would never have guessed. I tried to look relaxed.

We were off to a jerky start. I was doing battle with the plastic on the seat, my only comfort coming from the line of religious figures that were arranged on the front dashboard. The driver seemed nervous and drove at a snail's pace. There was a crunch as he changed gears. I tried to concentrate on other things, but then in doing so, noticed the length of the hairs growing from the top of his ears. He tried to make me feel at ease, but his running commentary was interrupted by his intense concentration each time the gear stick failed to engage.

'You can stay at my house next time you come here,' he told me. I pretended not to hear and looked out the window. The trip was a series of spasmodic stops and starts, with apologies from him each time it happened, as my back peeled off the plastic lining like sticky tape, and at least allowed a little air on my damp blouse before I was jolted back in my seat once again, stuck to the plastic. Finally, we arrived at the fort.

'I will collect you here in one and a half hours,' he said as he pointed to a meeting spot.

I looked up at the fort, noticing the steep climb. At the lower entrance were groups of men—dirty, grubby old men posing as guides and accosting tourists. I was an obvious target.

'I be your guide, ma'am.'

'No, thank you.'

'But you need a guide ma'am.'

'NO!!'

The stench of their body odour turned my stomach. I jostled my way past them finding myself walking faster, but they followed me, calling out. I ignored them and walked even faster. It was a steep climb and my hot pink blouse was noticeably wet and clung to me. An old woman sheltering from the heat under a piece of old tarpaulin tried to prop herself up with her makeshift walking stick—a broken tree branch,and held out her hand pleadingly. She looked hungry and tired and I pressed a gold coin into her deformed fingers as I dashed past. She offered a toothless smile of thanks.

I was relieved to reach the top and took a seat on a low wall in the shade. There was a slight breeze that I hoped would dry my blouse. My long, damp hair clung uncomfortably to the back of my neck as I caught my breath. From there, I could see the boundary walls meandering their way kilometres in all directions, with sheltering turrets at each outlook. The distant hills merged with the sky in the haze of the midday heat. It was an incredible fortress, and built in such a manner to be able to see the enemy approaching from any and every direction. I looked down to see yet another tourist running the gauntlet to pass the group of filthy vagabonds.

Tarun texted me. 'How are you? How is Jaipur?'

I answered back. 'I'm missing my travel guide.' I thought about my driver and the jerky ride I would have back to the hotel.

Below in the courtyard, a line of elephants stood patiently waiting to take tourists down the mountainside. The poor animals looked so tired after repeated trips up the steep hill to the fort. My peace was short-lived as I was pestered by more guides, so ended up attaching myself to the end of a British tour group, where I felt less conspicuous. Two Indian women in traditional dress posed for photos and smiled sweetly for the camera when paid, but otherwise turned their backs. Anything to get some sort of payment from the tourists.

The walk down was easier and my trusty driver was waiting. We made our way down the mountainside, following one of the elephants, my inexperienced driver travelling a little too close behind the huge animal. Like rain from the heavens, the elephant lifted its tail, and my goodness; I had never seen anything like it. Huge dollops of elephant shit fell from the sky just metres ahead of us. I wish I had gotten a photo of my driver's face. We braked suddenly and all his gods and goddesses on the dashboard hit the windscreen. He gave me an awkward smile, and rearranged the dash before continuing. I finally arrived back at the Diggi Palace, exhausted, with just enough time to change before Anu's driver arrived to collect me.

Once again, I had a delicious lunch and so enjoyed their company. With the samples in hand, I went back to meet up with Brigitte.

'I need to go and pick up some more shoe samples,' she told me. 'Do you want to come?'

'Sure.' Dare I send her alone?

'We'll have dinner when we get back. Sharma is coming to collect me soon. Maybe, he will know where we can buy a bottle of wine to have with dinner.'

It was just before sunset, and the bright golden ball hanging low in the sky reflected off the windscreen of the car, directly into our eyes, blinding us. Sharma pointed to a store. 'We'll go there.' We followed him in, but it was a liquor store—gin, whisky but no wine.

We were back in the taxi once again, and pulled up in the middle of a market.

'Come this way,' he was out of the car and directing us to follow. We tried to keep up with him as he crossed the busy road, dodging the traffic. However, it too was only liquor.

'Don't worry about it,' I told him. 'It's not important.'

We were both tired and just wanted to get back to the hotel. Back across the road he strode, while Brigitte and I made a mad dash between the traffic.

The sun had almost gone. Dust hung in the fading light. It was difficult to see and the streetlights were nothing more than a golden glow, shedding hardly any light at all. We made it to the taxi in one piece. I had to step back to open my door, but unfortunately, just as I did, there was a honking of horns as a bicycle rickshaw loaded with three passengers swerved to miss a car. The rickshaw driver missed the car, but could not avoid collecting me. My fear reflected in his eyes as he suddenly braked. The weight of the rickshaw, the driver, and his three passengers came to a screeching halt on my foot, knocking me to the ground. The bicycle chain dug deep into my leg. I had seen it all happening in slow motion, but was helpless to get out of his way.

The driver, an older man, was visibly shaken. He came to my aid immediately. His eyes were kind. He saw the tears welling in mine. By that stage, Sharma was out of the taxi helping to push the rickshaw off me, and I could hear Brigitte in the background.

'Barbie! Are you okay? Barbie, what's happened?

The pain was excruciating and blood poured down my leg. I was sure, my foot was broken. The old man spoke no English, but I could tell that he was apologising. It had not been his fault and I tried to convey this to him. My foot was already swelling.

Sharma helped me back into the taxi. 'Put your leg through here,' he directed me to put my leg through between the front seats. He got in the front seat and examined my foot.

'It'll be fine,' he said as he calmly massaged some cream into the swelling.

'Rub this in again tonight, and tomorrow it will be better.'

'Better! I think I might have some broken bones,' I blubbered, noticing the imprint of the tyre on my foot.

'This is special ointment,' he said still massaging my foot.

That night I took some Panadol and rubbed that special ointment onto my foot. I slept well, and in the morning... nothing. There was a slight pinkness where the tyre print had been the previous night, but no pain, and I could put my shoe on without any problem.

'All the swelling is gone,' I told Brigitte. 'That's unbelievable.'

Sharma arrived at the restaurant around breakfast.

'How's your foot?' he asked.

'It's all better. Where do I get this "magic cream"?' I wanted some to take home.

He smiled at me. 'You can get it at the markets. Did you look at the container?' It was in a very small plastic pot, and I had not put my glasses on to read the label. When I did, I read in disbelief 'Ponds Cold Cream'.

'You are joking.'

'No, it's true.' He was still smiling.

'But Ponds Cold Cream does not fix a battered and bruised foot.'

'No.' He waited for my response. The penny dropped.

'Do you mean, it got better because I believed it would?'

'Exactly!'

And to this day, I still have trouble believing that this actually happened, but I swear without a word of a lie, it is true. This is INDIA!

Wedding Invitation, 2006

No sooner was I back in Australia, than our move to Singapore was upon us. We found a lovely ground floor apartment close to the city. Our dining room windows opened out to fragrant frangipanis and a tropical garden and pool. I soon got to know my way around. My favourite haunt was Little India. I loved wandering around the markets, the familiar smells, the music, and of course, the brilliant colours of the women in their saris, all brought back memories of my trip.

Some months later, I received an email from my friends, Anu and Rohit in Jaipur. It read something like, 'In a few weeks' time, our daughter Shareen is getting married, and we would love for you to attend.'

AN INDIAN WEDDING!

It was around 3:30 am when I opened this email. I hadn't been able to sleep. I was so excited. Who could I tell? Bob was asleep. He'd be up by about 4.30 am. He did the early morning starts in Singapore to keep in line with business hours around the world. Could I wait for him?I looked at the email again. The wedding would be held over four days and I would need two outfits each day. What would I wear?

What's the time? Not long until Bob's alarm goes off. Make yourself a cup of tea. Calm down. I heard a sound in the bedroom. He's up.

'Guess what?'

'I don't know. Why are you still up?' He was half asleep, rubbing his eyes as he walked out into the light. Meanwhile I was jumping up and down on the spot.

'We've been invited to a wedding in India.' I followed him into the bathroom.

'India? Who's getting married in India?' he yawned.

'Anu and Rohit's daughter.'

'Who?'

'Remember the people I met in Jaipur?'

'Not really.'

I left him to get ready for work. He called later in the morning, after I had managed to snatch a few winks of sleep.

'What are the dates of the wedding?'

I told him.

'Unfortunately, I can't go. Everyone here is on holidays then, but you should go.'

'Really?!'

'Barb, you would love it. You'd better get cracking on your flights. Do you need a new visa?'

Getting an Indian visa in Singapore turned out to be quite an effort. Had all Indians decided to apply for new visas on the same day as me? The place was crowded, and as I took a number, realised I had 100 or so people ahead of me. I quickly grabbed a seat and ended up beside a young Indian man. We chatted as we waited.

'What's your number?' he asked.

'152. What's yours?'

'65. It's getting closer,' he said as he looked at the electronic board that showed 61.

'I doubt if I will get to the counter today,' I told him.

'Don't worry, you will be fine,' he said, as I saw 62 and 63 appear in quick succession. Finally, 65 flashed on the board.

'Come with me,' he said.

Up I jumped and followed him to the counter.

'Put your passport beside mine.'

I got a sideways glance from the Indian woman on the other side of reception. She lowered her head, and peered over the top of her glasses. 'And why would you be putting your passport out with his?'

'We are work colleagues,' my new friend told her. Well done. That seemed to shut her up and she put her head down and started processing his documents first.

'I'll wait for you outside,' he said once his papers were complete. My visa took some time.

'As for you, Mrs Carmichael, you will need a letter from your husband giving his permission for you to leave the country.' She lowered her glasses once again and gave me a satisfied look.

'Permission?'

'Yes. You are here on a dependant's pass. It is necessary. Bring it tomorrow morning, and your visa will be ready in the afternoon.'

I phoned Tarun. 'I'm coming to India.'

'When?'

'In a couple of weeks.' I was excited.

'We can organise your flights,' he told me. 'Family will be happy.'

I would fly to Udaipur via Delhi for a few days, before I left for Jaipur and the wedding.

'We can also organise your overnight accommodation in Delhi,' he added.

My next concern was, what was I going to wear? Of course, I had a couple of saris, but I could see myself unwinding as I got caught on something, or having it drop off. I had worn one years ago when I was on a cruise ship. I was 18. But at my age, I didn't really want to flash my pale, less-than-taut midriff. I found one outfit in Singapore, and decided to leave the rest until I was in Udaipur. I wasn't expecting to be going back to India so soon.

'Are you sure you are going to be okay by yourself?' Bob asked as he unloaded my luggage at the 'no frills' terminal of Singapore Airport. Shakti had booked me the cheapest flights.

'I'll be fine.'

'Call me when you arrive.'

'Okay.'

'Be careful!'

The overhead baggage compartments shuddered and rattled on take-off, and randomly during the trip. Once the seatbelt sign was off, hardly anyone remained seated. The flight was full of Indian families. One young man spent most of the flight walking his elderly mother up and down the aisles.

I arrived in Delhi feeling slightly nervous, alone in a city of 12 million people, a huge percentage of whom spoke no English. Once I collected my luggage, I made my way out of the terminal in search of the driver who had been arranged to collect me. There were many drivers holding signs with the name of the person they were to collect, but not one for me. It soon became obvious to the other drivers that my man had not turned up.

'Where you going, ma'am?'

'I take you, ma'am.'

'Which hotel, ma'am?'

There were a few things that I had forgotten since my last trip, one being the way Indian men just stare. It was hot in the terminal and the stress of being watched so intently was raising my temperature further. I tried to gather my thoughts, as the raw odour of sweaty taxi drivers closed in on me.

I phoned the hotel.

'Man is at airport. This is his mobile number. You call him.'

Hang on a minute. 'No, you call him and tell him I am here by the drink machine. I have long blonde hair and I'm wearing jeans and a blue shirt.'

I waited another half an hour and...nothing. As well, I tried the number I was given and it was turned off. SHIT!

It was my first time in Delhi. There had been no connecting flight to Udaipur until the following morning, so

Shakti booked me into a hotel close to the airport. An hour passed. I phoned the hotel once again.

'Driver cannot find you. He is at airport.'

'I know he cannot find me. That's why I'm calling you.'

Stay calm Barbara.

'Where are you, Miss Barbara?'

'I'm here exactly where all the taxi drivers are waiting.' Miss Barbara was having trouble keeping her cool. 'Please send another driver.'

'You Barbara, Ma'am?' I swung around.

'Yes!' I sighed with relief and as I turned, this little man grabbed my suitcase from the trolley and almost ran, past my fan club, with me trying to keep up.

'Slow down,' I called to him. He just looked back at me impatiently and continued at the same pace to the far side of the airport parking lot, beyond the taxi ranks.

'Here Ma'am.' He dropped my bags on the footpath.

Well, it wasn't quite the limousine I had pictured in my mind but a small old car, covered in dust, that had obviously seen better days.

'Hotel said they were sending a taxi.' I tried not to sound like a princess.

'No understand. Come!'

I opened the creaky door and got in the back seat—no seatbelts, of course. My 'chauffeur' meanwhile was battling to open the boot, and ended up throwing my suitcase on the front seat beside him. A cloud of dust filled the car. I was exhausted, but at last I was on my way, and looking forward to putting my feet up, and maybe having a little gin and tonic at the bar.

Shakti had told me that the hotel was close to the airport, so I wouldn't have far to go in the morning for my 5 am flight to Udaipur. After about 15 minutes, the driver suddenly turned right onto what was a type of median strip in the middle of the road. He pointed across the traffic heading in the opposite direction and said, 'Hotel ma'am.' The median strip was no more than a dirt track and he drove across it slowly to avoid the potholes. Oh my god. The hotel looked as if it was partially demolished. I could see something that looked like the main entrance, and several floors above it, but on either side, it looked like a bomb had hit it. Holy shit.

This had taken my eyes away from where we were in the middle of the road, now poised at right angle to the edge of the highway, about to cross three lanes of very fast-moving traffic. The driver started to nose his way out in a way that I have only seen in India. There was not a traffic light in sight. The first lane stopped for him, and gradually to the sound of screeching brakes and honking horns, we finally pulled up at the front door in a cloud of red dust. Where's that gin and tonic?

The dust settled more quickly than my nerves. The driver carried my luggage into the reception. It seemed that the whole of the hotel staff were there to meet me. I was checked in and taken to my room on the third floor. Of course, there weren't any lifts. The place seemed very quiet, and I wondered if I was the only person staying there. My heart sank when the porter opened the door to my room. It was bad. Really bad.

The room was painted a dirty mustard yellow colour. Or should I say, was painted a mustard colour a long time ago. Patches of olive green peeped through every here and there where strips had peeled off. Dreary dark maroon curtains hung unevenly over the window and blocked out any light, and dare I say, fresh air.

I checked out the bed. The brown blanket on top looked dirty and crusty. The pillows were about one inch high, and the sheets didn't have that freshly-laundered look about them and were worn thin with holes. I wanted to say 'take me to the Hilton'. I took a minute to think. My friend had booked and paid for the room, unaware of its state of repair, and I did need to be near the airport, and it was only for one night. Maybe I would just have a shower, go to bed early and watch some telly.

Then again, maybe I would save the shower until I was in Udaipur. The shower was all mouldy, as was the once clear plastic shower curtain; and the toilet—best not discussed. I looked out the window and there were construction workers just outside. Clang! Clang! Bang! Bang! Piles of bricks and rubble lay amongst the bamboo scaffolding and cement mixers.

Bob phoned. 'Everything okay?'

'Yes, everything's fine.' He would only worry, and there was nothing he could do from Singapore.

Tarun called. 'Welcome to India. We are waiting for you. I'll be at airport in the morning.' It was reassuring to hear his voice. I mentioned nothing. He also would be concerned. You can deal with this, I told myself.

The construction went on all night. I popped into bed fully clothed and waited for my early morning wake-up call. As it was, I didn't need it, as I couldn't sleep and was downstairs by 4 am ready for my driver. The outside temperature was around 8 degrees, and I wrapped my pashmina around me as we drove to the airport in the foggy darkness. I was relieved to be on my way to Udaipur. We flew into a spectacular sunrise and arrived there around 6:30 am.

I should have been tired, but I was excited to finally be in Udaipur. I looked around anxiously for Tarun as I came out of the terminal. My Delhi experience had left me rather shaken, wondering what on earth had I been thinking to travel alone. There he was with a big smile on his face, and as we drove from the airport, all the sounds and activity along the roadside brought back a familiarity that made me smile. In the midst of all this, Tarun began to sing. He had a very good voice. At first, I didn't know where to look. I had never had anyone sing to me before, but in India it is part of life. There are no inhibitions. He had a happy voice, and there and then, that morning, I felt safe.

'How was your hotel?' he asked.

'Oh, they were doing a few renovations.'

Jaipur, 2006

So, that was how we met. I had enjoyed being back in Udaipur with Tarun and his family. Tarun said he would be there to take me to the airport for my flight to Jaipur for the wedding.

In fact, the whole family arrived to take me to the airport. We must have looked a sight as nine of us ungraciously piled out of the small transit van. Tarun had insisted I sit in the front, and Mamma, Manisha, Shakti, Poonam, Riya, Rudrakshi and Mahipal somehow managed to fit in the back with all my luggage. I loved their informality, their family closeness and the uninhibited affection they extended to me.

Manisha and Poonam had gone to the markets and presented me with a box full of bracelets in colours to match my new outfits. I was going to miss this family. However, I knew I would be back. There was a special connection for me that had become even stronger in this visit. After all, I hadn't known them for very long.

'Text me when you arrive in Jaipur,' Tarun said as I hugged him goodbye. I felt my eyes well.

It was only a short flight to Jaipur. I did seem to have this recurring problem at Indian airports, where the organised driver did not turn up to collect me. On arrival, I was feeling optimistic as I spotted a sign 'Barbara' being held by a smartly uniformed driver. My accommodation had been booked at the Arya Niwas, where other wedding guests were also staying.

Relaxing in the back seat, and peering through the curtains (the more expensive taxis have curtains at the back) I had regained my confidence in Indian taxis.

'How far to the Arya Niwas?' I asked.

'Ma'am I am not from the Arya Niwas Hotel. I am from Umaid Bhawan.'

'I didn't make a booking there. I only made an enquiry.'

'Ma'am, I will call the manager.'

'There is no need. Are you able to take to my hotel?'

'Yes, ma'am.'

Thank god for that. I'd come to expect the unexpected. There's no point in getting disappointed. That's India. Just go with the flow, I thought to myself as I dived in the deep end.

I was greeted at the reception of Arya Niwas with a basket of goodies from Anu and Rohit, the parents of the bride. It contained all sorts of fruit, chocolates, biscuits and drinks; such a lovely gesture. I was also given the name of another female wedding guest staying there. Although I had come with all sorts of outfits, I still couldn't help but feel anxious about being correctly attired. I didn't want to look like I was going to a fancy-dress party.

After settling into my room, I made contact with the English guest Boo, who had a fashion business in the UK and had travelled to India many times as a customer of Anu's. She'll know what to wear, I thought.

'I'm not sure what to wear either,' she confessed. 'Bring your clothes up to my room and I can show you what I brought with me.'

That sounded like a good idea. 'Come up now, and I'll order some chai from room service.'

'You've got heaps of clothes,' she said as she opened her door. I laid them on her bed beside her pile of clothes. 'Any of these will be fine. I love the yellow. Where did you get these made?' She was checking out my outfits.

'Udaipur. I've just been there on the way here. I thought I might wear the yellow one tomorrow. It's a more informal day. What do you think?'

'I think that would be perfect.' Tarun would be pleased.

'What do you think of this?' she held up a purple and orange outfit.

'Looks great.' We made arrangements to meet at reception in the morning. I was relieved I would not have to walk into the wedding by myself.

Next morning, I was still feeling a little nervous and was on my way down to reception to meet Boo, when I received a text message from Tarun:

Look outside
It's so pleasant!
Sun smiling for you…
Trees dancing for you…
Birds singing for you….
Because I asked them all to
Wish you good morning.

I was touched. Not only did he sing, but wrote poetry as well! It was just what I needed. I didn't feel alone in India while I had my friend in Udaipur. He gave me confidence and I felt there was someone looking after me from a distance.

As I walked downstairs, I adjusted my scarf. Amazing how it just seems to sit perfectly on Indian women, and yet on me, it either kept slipping off my shoulders or I looked like I was being strangled by a bright yellow python.

'Very nice!' The man behind reception gave me a wink and a nod that gave my confidence another boost. I felt myself blush. Maybe, Tarun was right after all about yellow.

Once we had arrived at the farm, and I saw the other guests, I was completely at ease and mesmerised by the village women who had turned out in their best saris.

Festoons of orange marigolds hung in garlands at the entry gates. The day had been organised specially so that the local village people could join in the festivities. In the shade of a striped marquee, young men worked quickly, painting traditional henna designs on all the ladies' hands. Even the very young girls waited eagerly for their turn, before they received bangles and matching bindies. The women looked stunning as the sunlight caught the sparkle of sequins on their colourful saris, while the men were splendidly handsome in their free-flowing cotton suits and pointy shoes. Excited children ran about in their very best outfits, their hair all neatly brushed in place. Tables of food were laid out on the lawn.

Squeals of delight followed as platters of sweets were discovered. One young boy of about seven took himself off under the shade of a tree with his prize plate of gulab jamun, a popular Indian sweet made by soaking fried balls of chenna in syrup. The sticky syrup ran down his arms as he squatted on the grass, and trickled into his oversized shoes that were already covered in dust, collected in the merriment of a party on such a grand scale. The joy on his face will remain with me always as he savoured the last crumbs and ran his little fingers over the sugary plate for one last lick.

My digital camera was working overtime as I captured these magical moments, and a group of children gathered around me. I showed them the photo I had just taken, and then it was on for young and old.

'Me! Me!'

I realised that they had not seen a digital camera before, and to be able to see their image immediately on the screen filled their eyes with wonder. Groups of young boys lined up and posed, and then rushed over to see themselves in the image. The problem, of course, was that my camera card was soon full, and between deleting and clicking away, I was kept busy for about an hour. The farm manager, Yashwant, came over to me, making his way through the throng of children who had gathered around me.

'Do you want me to tell them to leave you alone?' he asked.

'Of course not.' I was enjoying their excitement.

Soon after, two beautiful Rajasthani dancers arrived. The first was dressed in blue with red and white trimmings, all heavily beaded. I was immediately in awe of the tribal choker and long earrings that framed her face. From the centre of her forehead, fixed beneath her headscarf, another stunning piece hung down to between her eyebrows. Her friend was dressed in red and black, also heavily beaded in white. She didn't wear all the jewellery of her fellow dancer, but a few red and white bracelets. Her face was that of a classic beauty, like an image from a Michelangelo painting, with the poise and grace to match.

Two young drummers started the musical proceedings, beating their well-worn instruments with what looked like walking sticks. Another two musicians wearing huge red turbans, one playing a flute and the other a tambourine, added another dimension to the sound. The girls joined in with a robust dance, their bare feet methodically keeping time with the beat as the bells on their chunky anklets tinkled.

The excitement was all too much for the villagers, and young and old joined in the dancing. Shareen, the bride, also joined them, her body sashaying left to right. Around her, the dancers and villagers gathered, and the pace quickened. Previously, I had only seen Indian dancing in Bollywood movies. To see the real thing was quite exhilarating.

An absolute feast was laid out in the shade of a huge marquee. Celebrations went on well into the afternoon and evening, with guests later dining at a city restaurant. I caught a taxi there with Boo but was feeling a bit queasy. By the time we were seated at the table I suddenly felt ill.

Excusing myself, I went outside for a bit of fresh air, and then hailed a taxi back to the hotel.

It was my first dose of 'Delhi belly'. Goodness knows what brought it on. I made it to my room within seconds of disaster, and then lay there thinking I was going to die. The world could have swallowed me up there and then, and I would have been helpless to fight back. Vomiting! Diarrhoea! Vomiting!

Somewhere I read, 'In India, taking your sense of humour is just as important as taking your Imodium pills.' At that stage, there was definitely no humour. The waves of stomach convulsions washed over me relentlessly until, finally exhausted, I slept. I felt lonely and vulnerable and wondered if I should call for someone, or a doctor. As the minutes became hours, my mind drifted.

'Will someone come looking for me in the morning?' I thought in the quiet of the night.

The bathroom was more than adequate, but I wanted my nice bathroom at home, and to curl up in my own bed. It was as bad as everyone said. Worse! No matter what you've been told, nothing, and I mean nothing, could prepare you for your first bout of Delhi Belly.

I awoke in the morning with a dreadful hollow feeling in my stomach and a fear of how I was going to make it through the wedding, the whole purpose of my being there. I felt weak, however, the stomach cramps had ceased.

I got a text message from Tarun. 'How are you this morning?'

'Not good. I'm sick.' His reply made me smile.

Fresh flowers for a very special person
With loving thoughts and prayers
To make your day lighter and brighter.
Leaving by donkey...
Arriving by super jet.

After my horrible night, it was a welcome, cheery note.

He called. 'Eat some banana. It will help.' That I did, and I felt well enough to go to day two of the wedding but not up to eating anything other than a couple more bananas.

It was the day of the Mehndi, and I didn't want to miss it. Before her wedding day, it is customary for an Indian bride to have both her hands and feet decorated in intricate designs with henna paste. Henna has been made traditionally for centuries from the leaf of a specific plant, ground into a powder and mixed into a paste with an acidic liquid such as lemon juice, and then applied from a cone-shaped bag.

On arrival, the bride was seated in a chair and two young boys took time in applying the henna on her hands up to her elbows, and her feet to mid-calf. All female guests were also treated to this cultural tradition. Mine was painted on my middle finger and a series of flowers and swirls joined with a bracelet on my wrist. The trick was not to let it touch your clothing or it would stain, so here we all were, wandering around with one hand outstretched. Once rinsed off, the design left on the skin was a dark, reddish-brown colour. Of course, on the darker skin of the Indian women, it looked stunning. Indians believe that the darker the colour of the henna, the deeper the love.

The garden had been transformed once again, with an even larger marquee. Deep blue carpets covered the lawn and white covered lounges and cushions provided seating. The vegetarian food was served from huge metal pots with warmers underneath. More overseas guests had also arrived.

'This is Barbara,' Anu introduced me. 'She has come all the way from Australia for the wedding.' Once again, in the late afternoon, cars ferried us back to our hotel to change for the evening event—dancing.

By the time we arrived back, a dance floor had been erected with the names of the bride and groom flashing on the floor. Garlands of marigolds were now lit with tiny fairy lights and the younger Indian women arrived in the latest sari fashion. Music was modern Indian, and the dance floor was full. Nobody sat down, and I soon learnt the meaning of the quotation from the movie *Bride and Prejudice*, 'Change the light bulb with one hand and pat the dog with the other', as I was instructed in the dance moves. The next day would be the actual wedding, and I was now feeling much better and looking forward to the festivities.

The ceremony and reception were to be held at the Rambagh Palace, described as Jaipur's foremost Royal Palace Residences. It spread over some 47 acres of manicured lawns and gardens. Peacocks roamed the grounds with the occasional show of plumage. I had, at one stage, thought I might stay there, but it would probably have cost me more than my flight from Singapore. Brigitte and I had taken a peek the previous year, as a treat after a long day in the markets, and we enjoyed the luxury of having a glass of wine in such regal surroundings.

I was excited at the prospect of getting all dressed up in my new red outfit. My silver necklace, bracelet, earrings and rings were just perfect—thank you, Bob and thank you, Tarun!

The guests were a sea of colours and styles, the younger ones in the latest fashion, flashing midriffs with sparkling jewellery hanging from every possible part of the body. The men were resplendent in their best attire: rich cream silk trousers and long shirts under beaded vests and golden mojaris (pointy-toed shoes). Of course, the colourful turbans completed the picture.

Shareen and Vinnie arrived in a magnificent golden carriage drawn by two white horses that were also decorated. Inside the palace, seated on a low stage, covered in colourful rugs, the scene was set with a group of musicians—all dressed in white except for their turbans. They entertained guests while the bride and groom made their way in. Shareen looked stunning in a heavily-beaded hot pink sari edged in green that sparkled under the lights, along with her beautiful jewellery. Vinnie was obviously proud as he guided her in his cream and gold sherwani, turban and mojaris. They truly looked the prince and princess.

Around 300 guests provided glamour and sparkle. I was in my element. I loved dressing in Indian clothes. They were so pretty and feminine and just seemed to shout 'celebration'.

'Where did you purchase your blouse?' I was asked.

'Very nice,' from another. Mr Krishna had told Tarun when he picked it up, 'I will be making more of this design.'

Once the formal part of the ceremony was complete, the doors onto the lawn were opened, where the wedding feast had been laid out. Dancing was again on the agenda, and I found so much pleasure in watching as well as joining in all the activities.

Back at the hotel, I took off my shoes and lay down on the bed exhausted but happy. It had been an action-packed few days. My first Indian wedding would remain in my memory forever.

Delhi, 2007

'Are you sisters?'

'Can I have my photo taken with you?'

'Where are you from?'

A group of young schoolgirls had gathered around my friend Pam and I as we visited the Red Fort in Delhi.

'It's because we both have long blonde hair,' I told Pam. We had only been in India a day, but already been asked these questions several times. After listening to my constant ravings about India, Pam had decided to join me.

We organised to be in Udaipur for Diwali, the festival of light, celebrated in autumn. I had been in touch with Tarun, and was excited at the prospect of introducing Pam to him and his family. The festival spiritually signifies the victory of light over darkness. The fourth day of Diwali is the Hindu New Year, and this festival honours the Hindu goddess of wealth, Lakshmi, to whom Hindus pray to bring them good luck in the coming year.

Being a popular holiday time in India, accommodation in Delhi was hard to find. One phone call led to another and we ended up finding an apartment that sounded perfect. I was wary after my previous Delhi experience. We were told the apartment was large, and although only one bedroom, the owner had offered to put a folding bed in as well. It all sounded fine.

However, on our arrival, it was not quite as expected.

'Looks like someone just left,' I noticed, as I checked out the items on the old-fashioned dressing table. Make-up and nail polish sat on a spillage of face powder. The room was full of other personal items, scattered on the bedside tables.

'This feels a bit weird,' Pam said as we explored. I plonked myself down on the faded lilac bedspread and almost did myself an injury as it was as hard as a board.

'There's the extra bed. It looks like a hospital bed. I'll take it,' Pam offered. It was 11 pm and we had just got off a long flight from Australia and were both tired. There's always a lot of organising to do before leaving family behind, and Pam had been burning the candle at both ends. She had been asleep before the seatbelt sign had gone off as we flew out of Sydney.

In the bathroom, toothbrushes along with half used soaps and shampoos had left their slimy trail. 'Yuk!'

'It's a bit creepy, isn't it?' I said as I pulled back the mouldy shower curtain. Memories of my last trip to Delhi crept into my mind.

There was a knock on the door, and it was the houseboy. He had made us a pot of tea. He popped the cracked, green teapot down on the table. I had been looking forward to my first Indian chai and watched as he poured it into two stained cups.

'Breakfast will be in the dining room,' he told us as he pushed the cups towards us. We both looked at the tea, and then at each other, but were so tired we just drank it.

We slept reasonably well, all things considered, although I did wake a few times as the bed did not surrender one inch of comfort. In the morning, we made our way to the dining room. The hallway was decorated with vases of dusty artificial flowers. We were pleasantly surprised when the lady who helped find the apartment called in to see us.

'How are you girls?' She was bright and chirpy, probably in her thirties, and dressed in modern designer jeans and top. Her name was Parul. We immediately warmed to her, and at that stage made no mention of our concerns regarding the room. Where else were we going to go? After all, it was only four nights.

She suggested local markets to visit, and offered to book a car and driver for us for the following day.

After a day at the markets, we caught a taxi back to our room. We hadn't realised that it was the day of the festival of Karva Chauth. On this day, wives pray for the long life of their husbands. We never did find out the day that the men pray for longevity of their wives. Apparently, on the previous day, the women must fast (poor things), and when the moon is full, they look at it through a sieve while praying for their husband's health. After that they are served some food by their mothers-in-law. On the day of the festival, the wives go to the beauty parlour, have their hair done, paint their nails, have henna painted on their hands, and generally make themselves beautiful for their husbands.

'It costs me very much,' our taxi driver complained, hoping for an extra tip.

Our day of shopping had left us exhausted. We'd had enough. Our legs were tired and we needed an early night. We stopped off on the way at a restaurant that Parul had suggested. The atmosphere was lively, with beautifully dressed women, many in red. We heard that wedding saris were often worn on this special occasion. I thought of the women back home, and how many would actually be able to fit into their wedding dresses year after year, and yet with a sari, one size fits all. We were in our jeans and feeling a little underdressed.

'Where are you from?' The women at the next table had been eyeing us off.

We smiled, and upon eye contact, one took the opportunity to get up and come over to our table. 'Are you travelling without your husbands?' she asked with a look of disbelief.

'Yes.'

'Is this normal? Are you sisters?'

'No, just friends,' Pam explained.

'How do you like India?'

'I love it,' I told her. 'I've been several times before.'

'Without your husband?'

I nodded and her answer was a look of astonishment. Although life is slowly changing for Indian women these days, most still lead a fairly protected life. They waved us goodbye. 'Enjoy your trip.'

We headed back to the apartment, loaded up with our shopping. We had a room key, but needed to ring the doorbell to be let in the main entrance. It seemed to take a long time for the houseboy to answer. Once in our room, I noticed the bedclothes had been crumpled.

'Pam! I think someone has been sleeping in my bed,' I remarked as we walked into our room.

'Really?'

'Yes, I made the bed this morning and now the pillow is all crushed like someone has been lying on it.'

'Maybe the houseboy is coming in to watch TV.'

'Let's see what happens tomorrow.'

The next day we were up and going early, as the car had been organised. Our driver, Subai, was a pleasant man and his four-wheel drive was most comfortable once we convinced him to turn on the air conditioning. Our first stop was at the Chandni Chowk markets. These markets are said to have been around for over three centuries and anything and everything was for sale.

'Take a rickshaw,' Subai told us, 'and I will wait for you.' A slightly-built young man cycled his rickshaw up to us. We offered to take two rickshaws, but there was no way that this wiry young lad was going to share his fare, so we jumped on board. Horns honked as he pedalled us into the oncoming traffic. We clutched each other as he slowly made his way across the two lanes of traffic on the busy road. A bus narrowly missed us.

'Oh, my god!' We were both pale. We got a mixture of stares, scares and hellos as we slowly—the emphasis being on slowly—made our way down the busy street, trying not to look at the man urinating beside us, however not escaping the very essence of it. The markets were divided up into different areas. The sunlight caught the sequins as row upon row of saris strung on wire blew about in the breeze, while silver jewellery tempted us to stop for closer examination. A labyrinth of narrow lanes and alleyways selling all manner of produce and artefacts ran off in all directions. Low-hanging electrical wires ran from one store to the next and were strung with banners, bunting and advertisements. Adding to the entangled wires were washing lines hung from the paltry dwellings above. In the food section, unrefrigerated goats' heads and other animal body bits were displayed as creatively as the huge mounds of pulses and spices nearby. Storekeepers waved cloth to discourage the sea of flies that the heat and smell of raw meat had attracted.

Women covered in black except for their eyes, cast their enquiring stares at us from the safety of their hijabs. I had decided to video our little journey by holding my camera low and not drawing any attention to the fact.

'We'll have a gin and tonic with our video show when we get back,' Pam suggested. Our driver pedalled us through to the other side of the markets and to the entrance of the Red Fort, where we continued by foot.

The fort was a calm respite after our ride. With warnings of pickpockets, we finally were allowed in after stringent security checks. Flocks of pigeons lined the rooftops, occasionally flying off in startled masses as noises from the nearby building site echoed off the walls. We were surprised at the lushness of the green lawns and inside came across a very old banyan tree, its tangled roots and trunk—an amazing sculpture of nature.

Further in, we caught sight of a large group of schoolgirls being led across the sea of green by their teacher who wore a blue shirt and electric blue turban. Suddenly, the dull, old walls of the ancient fortress came to life with vibrancy and laughter, as around 30 beautiful young girls, probably around 14 to 16 years old, and adorned in every possible colour, clambered up the worn marble stairs, their scarves flowing behind them, and their neatly-plaited hair sprouting golden marigolds. Their giggles of excitement rang out melodiously through the building.

A young man sweeping the stairs was momentarily swinging his rustic broom in thin air, as his gaze was taken by this bevy of young females. To me, it was one of the most beautiful sights I had seen, emphasising the colours of India.

Funnily enough, they too spied on us, and were equally taken with our long blonde hair, and posed for photos with us and enquired of our origins. And then the questions began. Maybe the fact that we were two women travelling alone made us more approachable. They were to become subjects of my paintings for my next exhibition, and their inspiration lingers still. Colour can be so uplifting.

Our driver was waiting outside the fort for us, and took us on a tour around Delhi and then dropped us off at the apartment.

'Looks like someone has been in here again,' Pam suggested as we examined our beds, and Pam went over and checked her luggage. 'Maybe we should call Parul and see what she says.'

Parul was horrified. 'I'll come and get you in an hour,' she told us. 'I have somewhere else for you to stay.' Although a bit cramped, we were very appreciative, and spent the last of our nights in Delhi there, before packing for our flight on to Jaipur.

Return to Jaipur, 2007

It was 4:30 pm and people were starting to drift back through the gates of the Diggi Palace, where Pam and I were staying in Jaipur. The garden was in shade. On the lawn, tables and chairs set with block-printed cloths provided a cool refuge from the hustle and bustle of the city. I took a seat and checked my phone messages.

'How's Jaipur?' Tarun had texted. 'We are waiting for you. How is your palace?' I was so looking forward to getting to Udaipur. Diwali was coming up and I knew we would be invited to join his family celebrations.

Renovations had taken place at the Diggi Palace since my last stay with Brigitte, and the dining room was now downstairs by the garden. I liked staying there. It was such an old building, and I found it a little *Fawlty Towers* in that you sometimes had to go downstairs on your way upstairs.

Three young men sat on their haunches weeding the grass while squirrels ran up and down the tree trunks. Beautiful green parrots feasted on bowls of seed.

Seated at one table were a group of women who Pam had referred to as 'the clutchers'. They clutched their bum bags even while in the safe bounds of the garden. Whether at breakfast, lunch or dinner, there they were clutching like some extreme advertisement for travel safety. In their comfortable walking shoes and identical short haircuts, they chattered away in German and then headed back out the gate for another bout of shopping.

'Gin and tonic, Madam!' My drink arrived with a side of ice. Dare I? So tempting, but being sick in India once is enough. I declined. Wilson, the manager, had kindly contacted Omesh, the driver I had previously used, and he was available for us.

As I sipped on my drink, the owner, a beautiful woman named Jakita, drifted by in an exquisite yellow sari. How do Indian women always look so cool, even on the hottest of days? Her jewellery was equally splendid—rubies and diamonds, at a glance, on her ears, and a striking piercing on her nostril. She directed the weeders. I noticed the floral underskirt of her sari had shades of mauve and purple that were revealed in the breeze.

I felt the first signs of mosquitoes on my legs as the sun lowered in the sky and more guests returned through the gates. My gin and tonic was refreshing despite the lack of ice, and I enjoyed it with a pappadum the smiling waiter had brought me. Pam finished her drink and then left on a little expedition to some nearby markets, and the plan was to go to the Rambagh Palace for a drink before dinner. Jakita told me that her dining room was open until 9.30 pm, so heaps of time to get back for dinner.

The day before, Omesh had suggested we visit both block printing and paper making factories on the outskirts of Jaipur. There we were able to watch firsthand the intricate process of block printing from an artist who had been working there for 42 years, following traditional methods centuries old. We were surprised to learn that the main ingredient in the making of some of the colours was rusty horse shoes. Yes! Horse shoes! I was astonished.

Horse shoes and rusty old nails were left for a period of time in vats of sugar and water, and to this mixture, other natural ingredients were added. Some of these included pomegranate and gum from the acacia trees. Apparently, the naturally high fluoride content in the local water was the way in which the finished product was set. Washed in this water, the pattern would remain colourfast forever.

The artist, a man in his late fifties proudly demonstrated his craft. He was dressed in typical Indian wrap pants in a deep mustard brown. As he mixed the individual colours, I noticed his hands, permanently stained with ink. Some pieces had up to 20 different blocks making up the design. He was working on a deep red bedspread with a border of elephants. The factory owner told us that the artist could complete the queen size bedspread in 12 hours. He was quick and accurate in his approach, and gave each block a thud with his multicoloured fist to guarantee an even registration. It was hot inside, and I wondered how often he had a break.

In the evening, Omesh had suggested he take us to Chokhi Dhani, a re-creation of a traditional rural Rajasthani village, on the outskirts of the city. Entry was 275 rupees, which included dinner. We worked it out to be around $A9. He hadn't thought to tell us that dinner was served on tables very low to the ground, and sitting cross-legged was the order of the day. Funnily enough, neither Pam nor I can sit properly cross-legged, and this caused much hilarity for the two young men sitting opposite us. Between us, it wasn't a very ladylike look. We tried to observe the 'use only right hand' approach. Easier said than done. Try buttering chapattis, breaking them up, and eating from tiny little leaf plates—their version of our paper plates, only moulded from dry leaves. Drinks were served in what looked like unglazed rough earthenware tumblers. Of course, we drank bottled water.

'Should we be drinking out of these rustic cups?' I had asked Pam.

There was no dishwasher humming along in the background, but a big bucket where the mugs were dunked.

After sitting in a somewhat awkward position for some time, my whole left foot was numb. I wondered how I was going to get up. I mentioned it to Pam who said, 'Yes, I have pins and needles in my legs as well.'

The meal was fully vegetarian and served by waiters who grabbed a handful and placed it on our plate. There were all manner of dishes, along with rice, chutneys and sauces. A communal cloth was passed around to wipe our hands when we were finished. Finally, sweets were served—jalebis, delicious fried circles of sweet dough. Slimming of course!

There were only a few tourists there, and Pam and I were a constant source of interest with our long blonde hair. Mothers pointed us out to their children and told them to go and practise their English on us, and have photos taken with us. Who knows where those photos ended up and what stories would go with them.

Once finished, it was a long drive back to the Diggi and Omesh drove cautiously, as there were many large lorries on the road after 10 pm. It had surprised me how many of the large vehicles had no rear lights or reflectors, appearing only as large moving shadows on the road. Mix this with bicycles, motorcycles (also with no lights), pedestrians, and fast-moving cars, and it was a recipe for disaster. However, we felt quite safe with Omesh. The previous day, he had taken us to his family home on the way to the fort and we had met his mother and father. His father had been in the police force prior to his retirement, and photos in full uniform adorned the walls of their living room. His mother served us tea and sweets before we climbed the stairs to the rooftop, directly opposite the Palace of the Winds and took in the view over Jaipur to the fort beyond. We felt indeed privileged to have had such a personal tour.

The Palace of the Winds was covered in bamboo scaffolding while the annual painting took place. This apparently happened after the monsoons; a bit like whitewashing, only in ochre. Monkeys scrambled along the rooftop, their bodies silhouetted against the afternoon sun, and pigeons fought for space on the turrets of nearby buildings. Below, people gathered around a fruit cart—pomegranates, bananas, lemons and limes—a colourful picture against the saffron sari of a young mother as she held her baby. Another in a hot pink sari, perched herself side-saddle on the passenger seat of a motorbike, a bag of fruits in her hand seemingly balancing her as the bike took off in a not-so-quiet fashion. The young man at the helm looked cool in his sunglasses, slicked-back hair, jeans and checked shirt.

Omesh beckoned us back down the stairs to continue on our way to the Amer Fort, sometimes known as the Amber Fort. It is situated in Amer, some 11 kilometres from Jaipur. We passed the trail of elephants doing their daily chores of ferrying tourists up to the fort, and also faced the cheery waving trunks of those on their way down the hill. I smiled to myself as I remembered the last time I was driving behind an elephant, while visiting the fort on my first visit to Jaipur. I had warned Pam of the many would-be guides who harass tourists at the entry, and I swear the same old man who I tried to outwalk two years previously, was doing his best to convince us to pay him to be our guide. I was sure it was him. I recognised his 'scent'—not easily forgotten. I don't think he had bathed since the last trip. We walked quickly up the steep path, and finally reached the shelter of the higher turrets, supported by carved marble pillars. The sight from there was truly spectacular. We were in the heavens, and no wonder it was such an amazing fortress, as we could see for miles and miles. Keyhole openings framed the distant mountains. I directed Pam to a chamber of mirrors that I remembered from last time; the whole of a huge room was tiled with them, and once candles were lit, the room became suffused with light. How romantic!

The fort was home to an interesting array of characters. Not wanting to be too obvious in taking photos, we did ask first before taking their photo, and in most incidents, ended up paying a small amount for the privilege. I didn't mind doing this, as I know myself that I wouldn't want someone poking a camera in my face back in Australia as I was walking down the street. I think that sometimes tourists forget that the people aren't just there for them to take photos, it's actually their home, and we should respect that.

Back at the Diggi Palace, the light was beginning to fade away when Pam returned from her little expedition, full of exciting news. She had been to the flower markets, and enthusiastically suggested I go back with her, as apparently, the bangle makers were in the little laneway nearby. Not needing much convincing, we were soon on our way in yet another tuktuk.The markets were crowded and the scent of roses, jasmine and marigolds were a refreshing change to some of the other 'nose teasers' we had come across. We wandered down the rows of flower vendors, and stopped at the stall of a beautiful young woman, dressed in the most colourful floral sari. Row upon row of threaded garlands lined her low table as she sat cross-legged behind it. What a picture!! I bought a couple of garlands from her and asked if it was okay to take her photo. The prices she quoted for the pieces were probably ten times more than she would have received from the locals, but I didn't mind as I captured the image. She proudly flashed the notes to her nearby competitors (mostly males), as her lips curled up in a huge smile. Each time I go to Jaipur, I try to visit the flower markets, and I have photos of her over a period of around ten years and have seen her grow from a young woman, into now a mother. About 50 metres on and down a little laneway, we moved to the bracelet markets. It was fascinating to watch as the craftsmen heated shellac and formed it into the shape of a bangle over the flame of a tiny gas burner. While it was still warm and pliable, pieces of coloured glass and mirror were pressed into it. Of course, some were made of metal, and others in precious metals. A young couple with a baby stopped to choose some bracelets. Pam and I smiled at the baby and said hello. The young man then passed the smiling baby on to Pam while his wife took a position on the floor beside a huge box of coloured pieces. Pam had her hands full, but the young woman took her time trying to match her jewellery with the striking orange and blue sari she was wearing. As we were finally on our way back to the tuktuk, I told Pam. 'This is the place where I was run over. Careful on the road!' It was about the same time of day—neither light nor dark. We saw a splash of brilliant saffron in the distance. It was a holy man. He was very tall and had the most striking orange turban on his head, together with a matching robe, and then a lighter shade of orange cloak. Silver-framed sunglasses and the red marking on his forehead left little of his face showing, as a bushy black beard and moustache disguised the rest of him. I found India to be full of these characters.

Jaipur to Jodhpur by Train, 2007

Daylight began to fade away and the sky was filled with tiny birds. It was just after sunset on the rooftop of the Haveli Guest House in Jodhpur as I gazed up at the Mehrangarh Fort. The colourful walls of the buildings of this city varied from lilac to hydrangea blue, depending on the play of light and shadow. Now, as daylight was beginning to fade, it was a deep sapphire.

As the sting of the sun slowly weakened, the sounds of tuktuks and beeping horns faded, and guests had begun to congregate on the rooftop. Waiters flitted about, laying colourful cushions, lighting candles and serving pre-dinner drinks. Fireworks crackled in the distance announcing the forthcoming Diwali, the festival of light. We would be in Udaipur for that celebration. Above the silence, the evening call to prayer echoed across the city from the dizzy heights of a minaret in the fading distance. The Mehrangarh Fort glowed as it silhouetted against the sky, as the light of day slowly disappeared below the horizon. Lights shone from the windows of the blue dwellings that sat in the shadows of the fort, and the last of the little birds rushed against the darkness. Each day was bringing us closer to Udaipur, and although I was enjoying Jodhpur, I was also eager to reach my favourite city.

During the day, we had visited a family of weavers in the village some 30 minutes from Jodhpur. Seemingly in the middle of nowhere, we passed a group of women carrying huge bundles of sticks on their heads. In the fields, colourful splashes of orange and crimson saris were dotted amongst the crops of chillies and vegetables. Huge lorries bumped along the dirt road, leaving it to the last minute to move off to one side and allow us to pass. Camels with their hides shaved in intricate patterns made their own pace, pulling wooden carts with all manner of produce. The camels chewed as they trundled along, and their drivers lay back on the sacks, sleeping.

Motorbikes and scooters zoomed by with three, sometimes four people on board. In the middle of a semi-cleared dusty field, the local village cricket match was taking place. Indians love their cricket. Mention you're Australian, and a big smile appears.

'You Australians champions,' one young boy told me.

On arrival at the village, a most delightful man, Roopraj and his wife Nanio, welcomed us. Most of their waking hours were spent sitting cross-legged on the bare ground, creating intricately-woven rugs using rustic looms made from crude branches. He explained how he had formed a cooperative with neighbouring weavers

'We work very hard,' he said, 'and we were only receiving a very small portion of the selling price of our rugs.' He pointed to a mound of completed rugs. 'Have a look. You will see the quality.'

Pam pulled out a predominantly red one. 'I think I might have to have this one.' Roopraj smiled proudly.

'This is our showroom. The local weavers all bring their rugs here now.' We followed him into a small thatched mud hut.

'We built it from cow manure and sand,' he told us. 'It keeps the mosquitoes away.'

The buildings had thatched rooftops over timber struts while traditional white paintings depicting village life, such as small handprints announcing the birth of a child, decorated the outside textured walls. Together, he and his wife demonstrated their weaving technique. As they did so, Roopraj's colourful turban danced on his head while Nanio's bracelets made music as she flicked her scarf out of the way of her nimble fingers.

Coloured threads tumbled out of woven baskets lying beside her on the earthen floor. With absolute precision, they each worked on their side of the loom, beating each row of colour with their weavers' combs. Pam and I both made purchases and Roopraj organised their freight, and promised they would be back in Australia before we were.

On our way back to Jodhpur, our driver took us up the narrow winding road to the fort, rising high above the city. From that vantage point, the famous 'blue city' is shown to its best advantage, almost blending in with the haze of the sky above. The fort was a maze of intricately carved marble and granite reception areas, the grander ones belonging to the king at the time. It would seem, from the information we were given, that the original king was quite a lad. We saw his bedroom, the bedroom of his legal wife, the bedroom of his illegal wives, and the bedroom of his mistresses.

'Blimey!' said Pam.

The light played rainbow patterns on the marble floor of the dancing room where, we were told, a troupe of dancing girls entertained him. His wife (obviously a patient woman) was not allowed in, but could watch from another room by way of a series of mirrors, permitting her to see what (or part of what) was happening.

Mehrangarh is apparently one of India's largest forts, and construction began back in 1459 at the behest of the original founder of Jodhpur, Rao Jodha.

By this stage of the day, Pam and I were beginning to feel tired. Our trip from Jaipur to Jodhpur by train the previous evening had been quite an adventure, and had not been without incident. We had left the Diggi Palace loaded up to the hilt in a tuktuk. On arrival at the railway station, we were unloading our luggage when a very tall, quite elderly man, dressed all in white, offered to carry our luggage. We showed him our ticket, not knowing where the correct platform was. He picked up our heavy bags and took off at a great pace with Pam and I struggling to keep up. We followed him up the stairs, across the tracks, down the stairs for at least 50 metres. As we huffed and puffed behind him, he carried on effortlessly, and then dropped our bags in the exact place for our carriage.

'Namaste!' His kind dark eyes thanked me, and then lingered a moment when I paid him.

There was a familiarity about him, and he turned back and smiled as he left.

Who are you? I wondered as I watched him go.

'Sounds strange,' I said to Pam, 'but I think I somehow know him.'

'Really?' she replied. 'Where from?'

'I don't know. It's just a feeling.'

We didn't need to worry about missing the train. India is not a place for the impatient; things happen in Indian time, which had become more apparent the more times I visited. The train was one and a half hours late. Obviously, this would make our time of arrival much later, so I phoned ahead to the hotel to alter our pick-up time.

When it did finally arrive, Pam jumped aboard and found our seats while I stayed with the luggage. Luckily, we were just inside the door. Our seats were opposite each other. A porter came around with crisp, freshly-laundered sheets and plump pillows, probably the best we had had the whole trip.

'Oh my god!' I let out a squeal.

'What's wrong?' Pam looked worried.

'It just hit me! The man who carried our bags IS the man who ran over me with his rickshaw two years ago!'

'You're kidding!'

'No! It's true. I knew something was familiar when I looked into his eyes.'

'How amazing is that!'

I am sure to this day that he recognised me.

This is India. If you are looking for a needle in a haystack, you are more likely to find it here amongst the millions of people than anywhere else in the world.

On the train, we made ourselves comfortable. Well, as comfortable as we could. Directly across, and constantly staring at us, was a very large man with a moustache. All these years later I still can't get over how Indian men stare at Westerners' fair hair. Without making eye contact, we set up our little bar on the table, all disguised in water bottles—Pam with her Pimms, which we called black currant juice and me with my holy water (gin). The staff at the Diggi Palace had made up some sandwiches, tasty little peanut butter numbers that had suffered from the heat and the train's late arrival. We got them out to have with our Pimms and gin with Melon Dew. There had been no other soft drink available on the station. What an interesting combination that turned out to be. We had a drink and downloaded photos from our day's travels on my laptop, creating a bit of a stir in the carriage. By this time, the man across the way had made up his bunk and he was lying down, but that didn't stop him continually staring at us. Finally, he turned his back. Thank goodness!

Two guys in the next compartment popped their heads around the corner and also started gawking. Trying to outstare them did not work.

The train rolled along in darkness, and the gentle rocking of the carriages was enough to make us sleepy. Cabin lights were lowered, inducing sleep. We stashed our handbags and valuables under our pillows. Soon the carriage was filled with the sounds of gentle snuffles and snorts, with occasional loud snores that worked up to a crescendo and faded, only to begin again.

We were almost asleep when the man opposite us suddenly sat up, burped, snorted, farted and burped again. Pam and I tried to contain our hysterics, meanwhile, he gained his composure with a few more throat-clearing noises (ones I would prefer not to describe), then lay down and was soon snoring again.

We dozed off until I awoke to find a group of men standing at the end of our bunks, watching us sleep.

'Pam! Pam! Wake up!'

Sleepily, Pam sat up and the men moved away.'Shikes!' said Pam. 'That's creepy!'

The train rolled into Jodhpur station in the wee hours of the morning. We made our way onto the platform, full of anticipation, but alas, no one was waiting, and we were pestered by both tuktuk and taxi drivers, eager for our business. This was despite the hotel having advised us that their driver would be there. He had even taken our carriage number and I'd confirmed that twice during the trip, when it became apparent that we'd be late. Yet, no driver in sight.

I called the hotel. 'Where is the driver? We can't find him!'

'He's there.'

'Where?'

'At station!'

'No! He's not!'

'We will send someone else. Will be there in 10–15 minutes.'

The platform was a sea of sleeping bodies, who didn't stir when the train arrived. There were people under blankets lying directly on the platform—homeless people who huddled together for shelter and warmth. We virtually had to step over these bodies to get off the station.

'Barbara!' I heard a voice. The second driver had arrived.

He grabbed my backpack and Pam's bag and headed off into the darkness, as he had parked on the other side of the railway line. He laughed as we passed a parked car.

'Your driver is in there, asleep. He will be in trouble with boss tomorrow!'

'Should we wake him?' I asked.

He shook his head mischievously.

The streets were dark and empty except for a group of men who sat on the side of the road, and a pack of skinny dogs rummaging through the rubbish heaps. Streetlights were dim, and we were grateful to be in the hotel's car. After all, it was around 2 am, something we were conscious of as we arrived at the hotel, and our young escort led us up four flights of steep, narrow stairs to our rooms. Pam's was directly below mine and both looked out to the giant structure of the Mehrangarh Fort, now in darkness.

'Is there anything I can get you?' he had asked.

'A cup of tea would be nice if that's not too much trouble.'

'No trouble. Come with me,' and he led us up another two flights of stairs to the rooftop restaurant and kitchen. It had been a long trip since our 4.30 pm check-in at Jaipur railway station, and the fresh night air was a welcome change.

The sky was ablaze with stars, and the shadowy image of the fort blacked out the immediate foreground. Our new friend made himself busy in the kitchen while we plonked ourselves down on the cushioned seating that outlined the low walls, lying on our backs and taking in the northern sky. Soon, the smell of spices—cinnamon, cardamom and star anise—drifted out from the kitchen and our cheery little welcoming committee presented two steaming pots of masala chai. Definitely a gesture above and beyond the call of duty.

We soaked in the night air and could easily have slept there, but crept quietly down the marble stairs to our rooms. I had a rather restless night, and awoke to the sounds of the early morning call to prayer, not long after I had fallen asleep.

The darkness of the night was lifting, making way for a new day, and I decided to watch the sunrise from the rooftop. A young worker was already sweeping and opening the kitchen, to the instructions of a charming man who later introduced himself as part of the family who owned the establishment. He explained that the Haveli Guest House had been in his family for many years, long before Jodhpur had become such a popular tourist destination. As it was, Jodhpur was the last stop by air as the airport in Jaisalmer was closed due to its proximity to the Pakistan border and the military presence there. Jaisalmer could only be reached by rail or car.

A whisper of smoke wafted out the chimney in the still morning air, and a waiter appeared by my side.

'Would you like chai, madam?'

'Thank you.' I needed something to wake me up.

The black iron tables and chairs of the restaurant were a perfect vantage point to view the whole city, including the many tiny blue dwellings that dotted the hillside. Traditional Rajasthani-shaped arches framed the view, creating individual vistas. Every conceivable space was put to use as steep, narrow steps, wound up to the rooftops of each dwelling.

A flock of birds made a graceful flight, only their silhouettes visible against the glow of the sky, and came to rest on the brass pinnacle of the old dome. The pink of the fort changed to orange as the sun rose and illuminated the village below.

As the sky lightened, the city clock tower came into view and the outlines of the domes of the buildings in the distance presented a magical image of an exotic sunrise. Of course, my camera was in overtime, not wanting to miss a single second. A tiny slither of brilliant, golden light appeared on the horizon beyond the city, far into the desert, and slowly rose until a fiery ball of light illuminated the whole of Jodhpur, as it bade the day welcome.

The red walls of the fort reflected the glory of the first light, and glowed in the shades of pink through to deep ochre. It was amazing to see the structure of the fort in this light, set high above the actual township with a winding road leading to the entrance gates.

On returning to my room, I saw the daylight view for the first time. From the window seat, I observed the beginnings of the day's activities at the huge well across the street. The familiar buzz of tuktuks permeated the silence along with a barking dog. The sounds of India!

A rose haze gently lit the horizon, merging from mauve into pale crimson as the sun moved higher. The white canvas of a marquee on the nearby rooftop glowed as it overlooked the ageing turret of its neighbouring building, its intricate carvings now covered in years of pigeon droppings and peeling paint.

Introducing Pam to Udaipur, 2007

'I'll be there to collect you,' Tarun had texted as we boarded our flight to Udaipur. The butterflies in my stomach began their gentle massage, and then took off in full flight as my excitement grew. It had been a year since my last visit.

I could see Tarun through the glass doors as we waited for our luggage. 'There he is,' I said as I tapped Pam on the shoulder.

'Where?'

I pointed and Tarun waved. 'That's him.'

I took a deep breath. If there were anyone who would understand my attachment to this place, it would be Pam. We had been friends and neighbours for many years, and it was her ear that had been continually bombarded with stories of my previous trips.

'Been shopping!' Tarun laughed as I dropped my bags to give him a big hug.

'It's so good to see you. How's the family?'

'Very good! And Bob, how is Bob?'

I introduced Pam and before we knew it, we were in Tarun's van on the way to our haveli.

'The lake isn't as full as last time,' he told us, 'but there is still lots of water. You will be pleased.'

'Great. I can't wait to see everyone.'

'They are waiting for you,' he said. I was there again, and all was good. I took a deep breath.

'Rudrakshi kept asking when would you be here,' he smiled and his head gave that familiar wiggle. 'She is very excited.'

My eyes met Pam's and nothing needed to be said. She knew what these people meant to me. We had travelled so well together, and could read each other like a book.

Horns tooted. The traffic was chaotic. Dust hung in the air.

'It's good to be back.'

He looked across at me. 'We missed you.'

A warm welcome greeted us at Kankawa.

'Barbara. Welcome,' Janardan called out as he saw me.

'I'll let you get settled,' Tarun said as he dropped our bags at the desk. 'I've booked a table at 8 pm over at Ambrai. We can meet there,' he smiled.

Janardan showed us to our shared room. It was up a set of narrow steep stairs, with a crazy little landing just outside the door. Actually, the crazy thing about the landing was that there wasn't one. You had to take one step down as you stepped out of the room, and then it did a sharp turn. It was most unusual. The uniqueness of this place was what I enjoyed.

'Love it!' Pam was also smiling.

Inside, block-printed indigo quilts over crisp, white sheets were a welcome sight. White-appliqued curtains draped the windows.

'Come on! Let's go to the rooftop! You have to see it.' I couldn't wait any longer. Kankawa is located on the edge of the lake and looks directly towards the Lake Palace.

'Oh Barb! I see why you love it!' Pam stood, mouth open, as she took in the view. I felt a calmness come over me. There wasn't a breath of a breeze. A small boat putted across to the other side without a sound. The haze of the afternoon sun hung low in the sky. I sighed as I took a seat and drank it all in.

'Chai?' I asked as Pam joined me.

'Mmmm,' she nodded, beguiled by the sight before her eyes.

In the late afternoon light, the walls of the palace were reflected in the lake. The heat of the sun had disappeared behind the havelis higher up and illuminated the turrets of the nearby City Palace.

'Isn't it magical?'

We both simultaneously took in another deep breath followed by a sigh.

'It's so peaceful,' said Pam as we looked out towards the distant mountains.

The magic of the lake drew me in once more—it captivated me. There, I could gaze into nothingness for hours without noticing the passage of time—it was like my soul simply rested.

It was as I remembered with the tiny shikaras moving silently through the water. I pointed out the Ambrai restaurant across the lake.

'That's where we're going for dinner tonight. We'll go by tuktuk,' I told her, 'and meet Tarun and Shakti there.' I had been enjoying seeing Pam's reactions and sharing my special place with my friend.

'Look!' Pam pointed to the adjacent buildings.Monkeys had just begun their daily migration to their secret sleeping spots and jumped and leapt with amazing dexterity from one building to another, and being a large group of around 50, provided quite a spectacle. The baby monkeys clung on desperately and amazingly, all made it successfully across.

'Come and I'll take you for a walk and show you around the old city.' I didn't want her to miss anything. 'That's a great bookshop,' I pointed out. The owner put his head out of the door and smiled.

'Namaste.'

'I've bought heaps of books from him,' I told her. It was a tiny shop, but crammed with all sorts of books from novels to larger coffee table picture books. He always had the latest Indian writers, and I'm sure that my heavy luggage was due to my purchases there. Further up the road, the tailor was busy in his tiny little space—just room for him and his treadle sewing machine.

'How long have you been here?' he called.

'One week,' I answered. He nodded his head, smiled, and his feet automatically moved back into pedal mode.

'He took up the hem on my trousers,' I told Pam. She was just smiling, taking it all in. The sting had gone out of the sun, and we walked all the way to the Palace Gates and back, buying a couple of strands of marigolds and jasmine for our room. We arrived back just in time to see the sun setting over the lake, and took in the moment with a gin and tonic on the rooftop.

It was a perfect evening with a myriad of stars upon a midnight blue sky. Tarun was already seated when we arrived at Ambrai restaurant.

'Great table,' I commented as we joined him. 'It helps when you are friends with the owner.'

Our table was on the very edge of the lake with direct views to the Lake Palace as well as the City Palace. Both were ablaze with golden lights and their reflections danced on the darkness of the water. Mouth-watering spicy aromas floated out from the kitchen. The evening was cool, and the moon rested high in the sky. A musician seated on a rug by the trunk of the mango tree played a gentle tune on his sitar. It was a perfect night to introduce Pam to Udaipur.

'Are you hungry?' Tarun asked surveying the menu.

'Shall I order for you?' We nodded in agreement.

'Shakti will come in around 15 minutes after taking his cooking class.'

He ordered the food as well as a glass of wine for Pam and I, and a Scotch for himself.

'So, how was Jodhpur?'

'Hot. Very hot,' Pam replied.

'Went to the famous Jodhpur sweet shop on our way to the airport,' I enthused. 'We have pista burfi, that yummy pistachio fudge finished with silver leaf, and pada made with cashew nuts. We'll bring it to the house.'

'Family will be happy.'

'We also tried some rasmalai, but couldn't bring any as it was too juicy to carry during a journey, so we ate it.' He laughed. Rasmalai is made from chena balls, served cold in a sea of sweet milk, flavoured with crushed cardamom and finely chopped pistachios. It is delicious, but very, very sweet.

'That is my favourite,' he rubbed his tummy.

'It's good you are here for Diwali. It is special celebration. All family is very pleased you are here.'

'Have you been to India before, Pam?'

'Yes, but only briefly to Mumbai. Not here. It's beautiful. I can see why Barb loves it.'

'You will come to our house for dinner before you leave.'

'Thank you.'

Our drinks arrived and Shakti appeared just as the dishes were brought to the table.

'How many in your class tonight?' I asked.

'Eight. All Australians on Intrepid Tour.'

The food at Ambrai was delicious as always. Bhindi masala (spicy okra or ladies fingers as it is sometimes called), saag paneer (Indian country cheese with spinach) and chana masala (chickpeas). Of course, there were chapattis on the side.

'What are your plans?' Shakti asked.

'No real plans. Maybe some shopping and sightseeing.'

'You should take a massage tomorrow,' Tarun suggested. 'You can relax. We have good place for massage. I can arrange for you.'

'Sounds good.' Pam was quick to answer.

'Come to my shop in the morning around 10.'

After dinner, Tarun phoned for a tuktuk to take us back to our haveli.

'See you in the morning.' He waved us goodbye. Our heads hit the pillow as soon as we got back.

Early the next morning, we were awoken by the sounds of enlightening music, and found out it was coming from the room of the French maharaja. There was a Frenchman staying at Kankawa, and according to his own research, he was a descendant of the original maharaja of Udaipur.

'Is that true?' Pam queried.

'I don't think anyone really knows,' I answered, 'but he comes here and plays out the part.'

He had introduced himself as such, and liked to be treated so, despite the fact that he looked anything but Indian, and on one occasion mentioned that he found Indian food too spicy. Five heavy gold rings pierced each ear, and his beard was trimmed in the fine lines of royalty. His appearance definitely demanded attention. With gold rings on most fingers, heavy chain bracelets and a massive gold buckle on his belt, he was indeed a picture of a modern-day maharaja, as he strode around with all the monarchic airs and graces of a king.

He had found fame in the local papers, Tarun had told me that he had hired a tuktuk for his entire stay, and had the normal cheap, plastic upholstery replaced with a zebra skin patterned fabric. Apparently, he lounged in royal style as he was driven around town, oblivious to the fact that he wasn't really being taken seriously. He said he had just come back from Nepal, and hence the music of the Tibetan monks. Although it was a bit of a shock at 6 am, I really loved the music—The Mantra of Avalokiteshvara, or Om Mani Padme Hum. For the next few days, the music blasted at sunrise, bidding everyone in the haveli a 'good morning'. I loved it so much that I felt compelled to find myself a copy once I got home.

However, one morning, it came to an abrupt end when a not so-spiritually-inclined German tourist asked him to turn it down, or was that off?

'Shut the fuck up! People are trying to sleep!'

Oh dear! Not quite the royal treatment His Highness was expecting, I'm sure.

In the early morning, the lake was quiet and I watched the sunrise. Our breakfast of fresh fruit salad with pomegranate was so tasty and served with our favourite, a pot of masala chai.

Tarun phoned. 'I have booked your massage. Come to the shop at ten. Here, the women massage the women, and the men massage the men,' he reassured me.

That sounded good to us, and we made our way there. The decision was for a body massage, and also the chakra, where oil is poured on the 'third eye' in the middle of the forehead. I had been a little apprehensive at first, but Pam reassured me.

'It'll be fine Barb! I've had these many times.'

'So, what do we do? Do we strip off to our underwear?'

'Yes!' she said. 'It's all very discreet—just a gentle massage.'

'Sure, Pam.'

We were shown to our rooms, side by side, and the first instructions.

'Take off clothes!'

'We leave on underwear?' It was more of a statement than a question.

'No!' the older of the two ladies pointed at my bra and panties. 'You take everything off!'

OKAY! Not quite going to the plan. In the individual cubicles, it was only politeness on our part that prevented us mentioning that the curtains did not meet. There was a huge gap in the middle. I found this quite odd in this land of fabulous fabrics. It was also a little off-putting when we were lying flat out naked, feet to the door.

'Hope there's no visitors!' I called to Pam in the next cubicle. 'How you going in there?'

'Good! Good I think! How about you?'

'Interesting!' was all I could reply.

There were two women massaging me, one on either side. They did not speak, and began on my legs, one on each leg. Robust thrusts massaged my legs from toe to top, so to speak. Should I have mentioned that I had short legs? My 'personal space' was diminishing fast and I suddenly wondered if I was about to get a full body massage. No thank you. As if reading my mind, they moved on to the rest of my body. I was oiled up like a pig for the spit. God, I wished I had stuck to that diet before the holiday!

'Body confidence!' I told myself. 'They do this every day.'

Deep breaths! 'Shit, I wish I were nice and slim!'

Now they were up to my boobs. What's that saying—slip, slop, slap!

'How you going, Barb?' Pam was having the chakra massage first.

'Oh, just fine,' I answered. 'You'll find out soon enough,' I laughed quietly to myself. There had definitely been nothing gentle or discreet about the massage.

We finished about the same time, and the women changed rooms, and I was prepared for the 'chakra'. What seemed like a tiny handtowel, or maybe it was a facecloth that was placed over some of me.

I mean you can hardly say, 'Cover me up, I'm cold!' when it's 40 degrees outside. However, I couldn't help but feel a little vulnerable with the open curtain.

The vessel of oil was placed over my forehead, and my head was then lowered over the edge of the 'slab', as warm oil flowed in circular motions onto my 'third eye'. It was relaxing, and seemed to go on for about 15 minutes, the oil running through my hair and, I noticed later, into a container on the floor. I wondered if it was the same oil Pam had. I really didn't want to know the full history of the oil. I didn't mind Pam's hair, but, oh my god, just don't think about it. As the oil flowed, my head was massaged, which was just wonderful, and my hair was gently massaged as well.

I giggled to myself, as I knew exactly what was happening to Pam. My massage was finished before hers, and just when

I thought it was all over, I was directed to a steam bath. The final experience!

The steam bath looked like something out of the ark, and the metal outer structure was painted a lovely shade of military green. It was one of those things you sat in with just your head sticking out. My mini towel and I were ushered across to the machine, and I was asked to 'reverse park', and winced as I lowered myself onto the metal seat.

'Oh, my goodness! Who else has been sitting here?' I tortured myself.

Once I was as comfortable as I could get, sitting on a sweaty metal stool in a claustrophobic metal box, the front door was closed with a creaky thud, and then I began the cooking process. I also realised that my machine was directly opposite Pam's cubicle, where she was having her massage.

'Don't worry Pam! I'm not looking!' I laughed as I diverted my eyes from the inadequate privacy curtain. 'Sitting in a steam bath in India does seem a little silly,' I called to her, as the temperature rose, and I melted into a pool of oil and sweat. After ten minutes, I had had enough.

'Let me out now!'

There were no showers there, so the idea was to wipe as much oil off as possible, and then go back to our room for a shower. In the meantime, I was wondering how on earth we were going to shampoo all the oil out of our hair. However, I did feel surprisingly relaxed, and the oil they used seemed to have absorbed into my skin, so it wasn't too uncomfortable to slip back into my clothes.

I waited while Pam had her steam bath and chatted away to the armless, bodyless head of my friend, as she poached in the time machine.

With our hair greased to our heads and tied in topknots, we returned to Tarun's jewellery shop. He smiled when he saw us, but his smile quickly dissolved into an outburst of laughter. 'You both look like you fell into an oil well,' he said once he could control his amusement.

'Do you think I could exchange some Scottish pounds?' she asked Tarun. It was a bit of a tall order here in the middle of Rajasthan.

'I'll call my friend, the moneychanger,' he offered.

He had a word with his friend and said, 'He's coming. Will be here shortly.'

Pam was able to change her money and everyone was happy. 'Now we need to get you back to your haveli.'

It was the eve of Diwali and celebrations were well under way, with most of the streets of the old city now closed off to all traffic other than motorbikes and scooters. Celebrations go on for three or four days and the streets are lit up with strings of lights. Tarun spoke to the moneychanger in Hindi.

'He said he will take one of you back on the back of his bike, and I will take the other. We'll have dinner at my house tonight.'

I knew Pam had ridden motorbikes before, so the prospect was not too daunting for her.

'Are you a safe rider?' she asked the moneychanger. He nodded.

So, with me on the back of Tarun's bike and Pam on the back of the moneychanger's bike, we made the trip back to Kankawa. There was no hair flying in the breeze, as we zoomed in and out of the narrow streets and alleyways. Our arrival was not necessarily elegant to our fellow guests, as we slid off the back of the bikes, hair dripping with oil. Never mind. The shower was wonderful, and we both slept like babies from then on. Even the hard, thin mattress of my bed did nothing to keep me awake.

That evening, we managed to get a tuktuk to take us to Tarun's house, and travelled through the back streets because of all the traffic congestion and road blockages. Lamps were being lit in the doorways and excited children waved as we passed.

Manisha and Poonam had prepared a sumptuous vegetarian dinner with palak paneer, a spicy spinach dish, chickpeas and salad, and finished up with a tasty sweet milky dish spiced with cardamom. They were delighted with our gift of sweets from Jodhpur, along with some gifts from home.

For Mahipal I had bought a torch with interchangeable lenses of dinosaurs. Needless to say, he loved it, and we spent the night turning lights on and off so he could keep trying it out.

Rudrakshi and Riya were very taken with our long blonde hair. Rudrakshi rushed off to her bedroom and returned with two brushes and gave one to Riya.

'Can we do your hair?' they asked.

'Sure,' I answered and Pam nodded as well.

They sat us down and gently brushed our hair. Next, they plaited it in two long braids, and then ran for a mirror.

'You look like sisters,' Riya laughed.

'I will take photo,' Tarun offered, while the girls giggled. Mamma said nothing but smiled a lot and clapped her hands as we showed off our new look.

I glanced over at Pam. She smiled. My friend had got it. She understood. This was family.

Pam left for Delhi the next day and it seemed quiet without her. We had such fun together. We had wandered up and down every alleyway and into every store. Our tastes are similar and it had been easy for us to be stuck in one place for hours if we hit on something special.

I missed her that night as I sat up on the rooftop. Spasmodic blasts of firecrackers had continued to pierce the quietness, as the smell of the smoke swirled high and then hung low in the air. In the distance, the Monsoon Palace glowed from its position high on the nearby mountain ranges. Downstairs, in the courtyard, a young boy was lighting the many little oil lamps.

Nearby, at the entrance to each dwelling, the doors were wide open and rows of small terracotta oil burners lit up the narrow streets. Excited children played and set off their firecrackers, screaming with joy as they ran for safety, while unsuspecting passers-by squealed with fright. Also decorating the doorsteps were traditional Diwali greetings painted in ochre and white. I heard the theme music of

Octopussy coming from a nearby restaurant. The long blue and red boat glided slowly around the Lake Palace, shedding its reflection, as it barely stirred the surface.

Further along, the more traditional Bollywood music echoed in the winding street. Storekeepers chatted in the laneways, all dressed in their best for the occasion. The streets in the market were strung with lights, criss-crossed with decorations, as families walked and greeted each other. I looked up at the entanglement of electric wires, and kept my fingers crossed that it all stayed in place safely. It had been a long day. I slipped away for an early night, as I wanted to be up for the sunrise.

And what a beautiful sunrise it was. After breakfast, Tarun arrived on his bike to take me to his shop on the Palace Road. I was no longer nervous on his bike. I had come to a point where I gave myself permission to relax and enjoy, and put my fears behind me. I no longer clutched him around the waist, but hung onto the bar behind me. In fact, he had a new Enfield that he was most proud of and it was faster and smoother than the old one. As we rode, I waved to his neighbouring storeowners, who were busy decorating the outsides of their shops with garlands of golden marigolds and leaves. The mood was festive. I helped Tarun decorate his store with long lengths of threaded marigolds hung in loops. It must have been a busy time in the flower markets. 'Can you pass me the string and scissors?' he asked from the top of the ladder as he tied off the last loop.

We stood back to admire our handiwork. Tarun looked at the neighbours' windows, and then back at his window. 'Ours is the best,' he smiled, and gave his head that little wiggle. 'Come,' he beckoned towards the bike, 'I will take you to the temple so you can see the Maharana. Today is the day he goes to the temple. All the people gather to see him.' He took me to a vantage point. 'This is a good place to watch.' He stopped the bike and let me off. 'I'll be back to get you in half an hour.'

The Maharana arrived in one of his open-roofed cars, part of his famous automobile collection. Led by his soldiers and accompanied by his family, he was given a rousing royal reception by his followers. His grey hair and beard looked quite distinguished against his dark skin and a brilliant red turban. People lined up in two queues to enter the temple after him, the women in one line and the men in another. It was such a colourful sight, as the women were all in their best saris. Jewellery sparkled in the sunlight, as they loyally stood and waited for their ruler.

In the afternoon, I took a boat ride around the lake. It was great to be up close to the Lake Palace and to see all the buildings along the water's edge. The small tour boats sat low in the water, and I had the unusual feeling of being below the water line.

That evening, Tarun told me to walk to the jewellery shop to meet all the family. Each night, the storekeepers along the way took an interest in what I was wearing.

'Very nice, Aussie Barbie,' the man on the corner called as I began my stroll to the shop. Already, the streets were alive with the sounds of firecrackers—some very pretty decorative ones, and others just one large bang!

It reminded me of my childhood, just as many things there did. Guy Fawkes night was still legal when I was a little girl in the country, and we would go to my aunt's house and have a huge bonfire.

Tarun arrived with the family in tow—all beautifully dressed, and he himself in a suit with a white shirt, and a red silk scarf around his neck. Very handsome!

Rudrakshi was first in the door, running to me with a big hug. She looked stunning in a white sequinned outfit with tiny little silver bell earrings and matching necklace. I hadn't been sure what to wear, and settled on my cream silk trousers together with white top and my new green scarf. And, of course, heaps of jewellery. I love getting all dressed up for these occasions.

Manisha and Mamma were in pink, Poonam was in a brilliant orange, and Pinki, the wife of Tarun's cousin, came in fire-engine red. Poonam had dressed Mahipal in white trousers with an apricot coloured long shirt, even with apricot laces in his shoes. He looked quite angelic, but appearances can be deceiving. Riya looked all grown up in a purple and white two-piece outfit.

Pinki set about preparing a place for the family to pray and had placed a red cloth on the floor, on which she arranged sweets, garlands of flowers, and lit a candle. Raj, Tarun's father, arrived looking most distinguished, and once Shakti came in the door, we all sat around in a circle holding hands. I felt so privileged to be a part of this family event. We prayed to Lakshmi for the prosperity of their businesses and health of their families.

'Now we will go to the rooftop of the Spicebox,' Tarun told me. 'We have some fireworks.'

The rooftops were very close together, and the only protective edge around the top was a low wall at about seat height. I could not help but feel a little vulnerable as I noticed the crowds on neighbouring buildings shooting their individual pyrotechnic displays off into the sky above our heads. My ears rang with the sounds of the close-range explosives. Mahipal was running here and there, and my heart was in my mouth, as he leaned over the edge looking into the street. Scared street dogs ran with their tails between their legs and yelped into the night with fright.

We had a bag of fireworks to let off, and once again, Mahipal was in the thick of it, grabbing the pieces from the bag as he held a flaming stick in the other hand.

'Mahipal!' His name was called as he got dangerously close with the stick or threw a firecracker too close. 'No Mahipal!'

'Mahipal, get away from the edge. You'll fall over.'

Poonam looked at me and rolled her eyes. Mamma just smiled and shook her head knowingly. She had raised two boys herself.

'He's a typical boy,' I told her. The air was thick with the smell of gunpowder. I hoped it wouldn't affect Mamma's breathing. She was already a little out of breath after climbing up the steep stairs.

The distance from one rooftop to another was no more than a few metres. Skyrockets were being fired from the nearby buildings into the night sky and ash fell and landed on neighbouring buildings. There was a scream, and I turned to see that Pinki's sari was alight. It was my worst nightmare. There was no fire extinguisher, blanket or anything to wrap around her to smother the flames. I quickly ran over with my bottle of water that I carry everywhere with me, and poured it over her. Luckily, it was full. Dripping with water, she smiled and thanked me. She was unmistakably shaken. Unfortunately, it was one of her favourite saris.

'Thank you.' Tarun came over once he had checked on Pinki. 'Just as well it wasn't your holy water,' he said and laughed.

'I could do with some holy water now,' I told him taking a deep breath.

Once the fireworks were over, Tarun walked me back to Kankawa. A frightened cow was huddled as close as she could to a corner in the nearby alleyway as the explosive sounds echoed off the ancient walls. I couldn't blame her. The air was polluted with thick smoke.

'See you tomorrow,' Tarun called as he turned to head back.

Once in my room, I lay on my bed. That was enough excitement for one day, I told myself as I poured that much-needed glass of holy water with a splash of tonic.

Conversations

People may wonder why I went back to the same place time after time. On each trip I managed to discover something new. I spent time. I sat. I watched. I breathed it in. There were days when the air was filled with the fragrance of sweet jasmine, and others when the smell of raw sewage turned my stomach. It didn't matter because India had captured my heart.

India's colourful. It's dusty and dirty. It's joyful. It's noisy but calming. It's frustrating but rewarding. It's relentlessly hot with temperatures reaching 50 degrees, but a great place to chill. Time passes at a pace that is of its own making. It's a place to learn patience—a place of smiles and a place of sadness. How can it be all of these things? It seemed the more times I went, the more I managed to let my mind and my soul float uncompromisingly in the sea that is India, and I gave it permission to be swept away by the current.

Once I returned home, I would read passages from my diary; how each experience had affected me, and what I had been thinking at that particular time. Often, I surprised myself. Was that really me?

I compared my diary entries to the process of painting. For me, painting was like meditation. I could completely lose myself in what I was doing, and then the next day, I would look again and think, 'Did I do that?' Sometimes I didn't even remember how I had done it, as I had become so involved in the moment. India had a similar effect on me.

Over the time, Udaipur had become my second home and Tarun and his family were part of my family. No matter how often I went, I still found the magic, the mystery and then, the longing to go back.

Some travellers go to India seeking to 'find themselves', to be transformed, without really looking beyond themselves. Others convert their foreign currency and then, feeling rich in rupees, forget their manners and the fact that they are guests in a foreign country. Many a time I have cringed when I've heard a tourist haggling over 10 or 20 rupees. However, I also believe in karma, and this country is the home of it.

In India, there is so much to learn. If you leave your blinkers on, you will obviously still see many beautiful things, but you will miss the possibilities.

I spent a lot of time sitting with Tarun in his shop. We talked nonstop about everything.

'Was your marriage to Manisha arranged?' I asked, and then stopped, worried maybe that this was private. He sensed my awkwardness and leaned forward, resting his hands on the table. He stretched his long fingers. 'In India it's like this,' he began. 'We have arranged marriages. It's our custom.'

I picked up my umpteenth cup of chai, and settled back in my chair. The air conditioner whirred, struggling with the high temperature outside.

'My parents chose Manisha for me. I was very lucky.'

'How did they choose?' I couldn't imagine my parents choosing my husband.

'Numerology is very important,' he explained moving his cup around on the table. 'An astrologer can predict the success of a match using birthdates, even the time of birth. Also, my parents made sure that we liked each other.' He smiled. 'I liked her very much.'

'Your parents knew you well.'

I thought of all the things that would have been taken into account. In India, the bride moves into her husband's family home, as would the wife of the groom's brother. It's important for everyone to get along. Manisha and Poonam, Shakti's wife, were best friends. They went to the market together. I longed to see them riding double on their scooter with the scarves of their saris flying behind them. They had fun together, ran the house together and had the utmost respect for their in-laws.

'I'm glad they chose Manisha,' I told him. 'I like her very much as well.'

He gave his head a little wiggle and grinned at me. Occasionally when a foreigner would come into the shop, he would encourage me to do the selling. 'They don't try to bargain as hard with you,' he laughed. I had noticed the rudeness of some customers. I admired Tarun's attitude. He was never rude. If they said, 'I can get for better price down the road',he would answer, 'That's a good price. You should go there.' They would look at each other in surprise and not know what to say next. He would simply shrug and continue to polish the rings laid out in front of him.

As I sipped the last of my tea, a trumpet blasted outside followed by beating drums. The shop door was closed to keep out the dust and traffic noise as well as the heat. Tarun parted the curtains to see what was happening in the street. He took a sip of his chai. Dust settled as a motorbike zoomed past. A skinny dog momentarily raised its head off the doormat, overcome by the soaring temperature.

'It's a funeral procession,' he said, as he stood closer to the window. I could see through the open curtain. A man draped in white was being carried high on a bed of flowers, his face exposed. He was an older man. The sight of his face took me by surprise. I wasn't used to seeing a dead person being carried through the streets. A group of men followed in a reverent march to the beat of a drum, their heads bowed in respect. I had read that when a person dies, he or she is taken in a funeral procession to the cremation ground. If the deceased is quite old, a band leads the procession. The eldest son, or a close relative lights the funeral pyre.

'Are you okay, Barbie?' I could feel Tarun's eyes on me.

'I'm fine.' I looked back at him. However, the image of the old man lingered. He quietly closed the curtain and we sat in silence while I finished my chai.

'Tell me about some other customs.' I was keen to change the subject.

'Do you know about Rakhi?' he asked taking another sip of his tea. 'It is also known as brother–sister day.'

'No, what is that?'

'Raksha Bandhan is a Hindi tradition. It means "bond of protection".' A sister ties a cotton bracelet on her brother's arm.' His voice was suddenly serious. 'In return, he promises to always protect her.' He was quiet for a moment.

'What a beautiful custom,' I said.

'It is mostly sister–brother but can be friends as well. It is the sister that asks the brother.'

'Should we do Rakhi?' I shyly asked. I hesitated. Maybe, I had overstepped the mark. His eyes lit up. 'Of course we can,' he smiled. I felt the warmth of his smile as he took my hand. 'You are now my sister. It's official.' He looked me in the eye. 'I will protect you.'

He stood up suddenly. 'Tonight we will celebrate.' I felt overwhelmed. Even though I didn't know it at the time, that simple moment was a huge turning point in our relationship. From then on, he would always introduce me as his sister. I think he even enjoyed the look of surprise on people's faces when he did.

'So, what else should I know about my Indian brother?' I was keen to know everything.

'Hindus fast one day each week, depending on their god,' he told me.

'So, what is your fasting day?'

'Wednesday. I fast every Wednesday, and that day is dedicated to Lord Krishna.'

'What if something comes up, like a dinner or something? Do you still fast?'

'Yes, of course. Wednesday is a special day in Hindu religion. People start their new businesses on a Wednesday. It is the best day.'

'Do you eat anything at all?'

'Very little,' he answered, 'but our bodies are used to it.'

'I remember going to your uncle's house in Jaipur,' I told him. 'They were all fasting.' I recalled being invited for dinner and I was the only person eating. It did feel rather strange, and I felt bad that his poor wife had to cook for me when she was fasting herself.

The young chai-wala came back and collected our empty glasses.

'Would you like to go to Asha Dham and see Sister Damian this afternoon?' Tarun asked.

'Oh yes,' I replied straightening in my seat. 'I have some donations for her.' When I had first met Sister Damian, she was caring for 40 people in rundown grounds on the other side of the lake, close to several huge hotels. I was struck by the contrast between them, but India is like that.

That afternoon, we took Tarun's motorbike and stopped at a wholesaler on the way and I bought huge bags of tea and biscuits. When we arrived at Asha Dham, the people rushed forward as the guard unlocked the gates.

'Tarun! Tarun!' they called and then waved at me. I had managed well, holding a huge bag in each hand, as well as a box on the seat between us. 'Well done,' he laughed as he took the packages from my hands. I had come a long way from my first ride on his bike.

There was a woman lying on the ground crying uncontrollably. Tarun went over, put his hand on her shoulder and spoke quietly to her in Hindi. She settled. 'What's wrong?' I asked as we carried the bags of tea and biscuits into the kitchen.

'Her family dropped her here. They cannot care for her any longer.' In India, there is a harshness towards women that I find difficult to come to grips with. I was told the story of the young woman who Tarun had found wandering the streets, lost and in a state of shock. At the time he found her, she was in such a state of mind that she couldn't speak. Each day, he went to visit her and gradually he gained her trust and she began to tell him her story. She had been picked up off the street in her village by a truck driver, and then hundreds of kilometres later, after suffering all sorts of indecencies, was pushed out of the door onto the streets of Udaipur.

'It took some weeks,' Tarun told me, 'but slowly, slowly, I was able to find her village, and then her father. I paid for his bus fare here to collect her.'

Life is not easy for many in India, especially the poorer women, who labour on the building sites and on the roads. It is the women who tend the goats, who work the fields and fetch the water. Those same women cook and clean, and often have a small baby strapped to their back. I feel for them, but I can't even begin to understand their great strength or their weariness at the end of the day.

As I stood there, looking at those abandoned women, I was reminded of the movie *Water*. It is the last of a trilogy by Indian director, Deepa Mehta, exploring the plight of widowed Indian women. The movie was set in 1938, and told the story of women who were sent to the town of Benares when their husband died. The same women who had cared for their husband and family, as well as working, cooking, cleaning, were shunned by their family, as it was seen as the fault of the wife if the husband died. With shaved heads, and wearing white, they begged for food and had no contact with their families.

I was horrified to find that these practices still continue in parts of India, and found an article on the BBC, 'The Indian town with 6000 widows' by Anthony Denselow on the town of Vrindavan, from May 2013. He writes:

India is jam-packed with holy sites and pilgrimage destinations. But few places are as closely associated with the deity Krishna as is Vrindavan, on the banks of the Yamuna, a few hours' south-east of Delhi. But Vrindavan has its darker, less-loving side—it is known as "the city of widows".

As I stood there, I heard the gentle voice of Sister Damian as she made her way through the crowd that had gathered around us.

'Tarun, welcome Tarun.'

In her sixties or seventies, she's small in stature but has the face of an angel. She has a kindness and a way with people that can only be described as a god-given gift. The number of people accommodated at Asha Dham had more than tripled since my last trip and resources were at the mercy of charitable businesses and individuals. I made myself a promise that I would try to do something to help before my next visit.

One woman had rushed up to me all excited, her hands covered in cow manure as she was in charge of making fertiliser. Please don't hug me, I thought to myself. She spoke excitedly to Tarun in Hindi. He looked at me amused.

'What did she say?'

'She said she would like some earrings like yours.' I was wearing a rather nice pair of silver earrings. 'Here, give them to her.', I said.

'No, no. You cannot just give to one. They will all want earrings,' he laughed.

Sister Damian took my hand in hers. 'Come, let me show you what we are doing.' She led me up the stairs, past some bedridden women. 'We try to make them as comfortable as we can,' she told me as she waved to them. One raised her blanket to expose the fact that she had no legs. Another called out pleadingly from behind locked doors; her wild dark eyes wide open, as if possessed.

'Some are too seriously affected to be able to roam the grounds freely,' she explained, her eyes sad. There is no real place for these women in India if they come from a poor family. 'No one wants to marry them, and their families cannot afford to keep them if they cannot work,' she continued.

'Some end up on the street, and that is when we find them and bring them here.' I looked around. Some were young girls and others old ladies. 'Here, at least they are fed and clothed, and also, they are safe,' she told me, wearied by the weight she carried on her ageing shoulders.

In the meantime, Tarun had been sitting in the kitchen speaking to one of the helpers. We joined him for chai. 'Can you come to the police station with me tomorrow, Tarun?' Sister Damian asked.

'Yes, of course.' He gave her a caring look.

'I go with her when she needs extra support,' he said. 'It's not easy for her.'

When we walked back to his motorbike, the people gathered around us once again. Tarun said goodbye, naming those he knew. He had made a difference to their lives and despite their levels of mental illness, they were aware of this. I felt very proud of my friend as we rode out through the gates, and looked back as the guard locked everyone in.

It doesn't take a lot to make a difference in someone's life but first you have to care. He cared.

On the way back, he dropped me off at the top of the lane to Kankawa. I was thinking about what I would wear that night when I heard a familiar voice. It was an American woman I had spoken to in Fabinda in Delhi. She had asked me where I had bought my linen trousers. I turned around and she recognised me.

'Hi, how are you?' she greeted me. 'Fancy seeing you here.'

'Are you enjoying Udaipur?' I asked.

'Lovely. I don't suppose you know of a good jewellery store? We have been invited to dinner in a hotel across the lake tonight, and I've heard it's quite upmarket. Udaivilas, do you know it?'

'I've heard it's quite amazing. I'm actually going there myself tonight.' Tarun had said he would take me to the gallery there. I don't know whether I was imagining it, but that seemed to take the wind out of her sail a bit.

'I'm looking for some jewellery to wear.'

'Actually, my friend has a jewellery store 50 metres down the road. Would you like me to take you there?' She nodded. I called Tarun as we walked. 'Lucky is minding the store,' he told me. 'Call me if you need anything.'

Lucky gave me a huge smile when I came in. He's a young man around 20 years old, and a gentle giant at over six feet tall. I gave him a wink as I showed the lady to the glass cabinets.

'I'll know it when I see it,' she said as she leaned over the stock looking for that special piece.

'This is perfect, except I would rather prefer a bracelet and earrings than a necklace.' She pointed to the item. 'Do you have a bracelet like this?'

I looked at Lucky and he shook his head.

'Maybe we can make you a bracelet and earrings out of the necklace,' I suggested just as Tarun came in the door.

'Can you change this into a bracelet and earrings?' I asked.

He turned to the lady. 'When do you need it by?'

'We're being collected from our hotel at 7 pm,' she said checking her watch as it was already 5 pm.

'I'll call my jeweller,' said Tarun, and he was on the phone in an instant.

'No problems. I will deliver it to your hotel before then. Which hotel?'

She gave directions. 'That's near Barbie's hotel.' He looked at me. 'I'll collect you at the same time and we'll go to the gallery.'

'Good.' The lady was pleased. We all went our separate ways, and I took some chai on the rooftop before I showered and got ready. I decided on my new pink silk kurta and silk trousers. I made my way to her hotel close to the nominated time. Tarun was already in the lobby, and we called her room. She came down with her husband, all beautifully dressed for their dinner. The bracelet and earrings were a perfect match with her outfit. She looked at me in my silk kurta and pants. 'Where are you off to?'

'We're off to Udaivilas as well. Tarun is taking me to the art gallery.'

'We have a car. Come with us.'

'No, it's okay. I have a lift.'

Tarun had gone across the street to drop something else off and I pointed to his motorbike. She looked disapprovingly at her husband. 'Darling, she can't. Tell her to come with us.'

'Barbie,' I heard Tarun calling, as he started up his motorbike. The look on her face was worth bottling.

'See you there.' I waved and walked over to the bike.

'No, come with us,' she offered again.

By that stage, I was on the bike. Being a bit naughty, Tarun gave it an extra rev as we took off.

'Did you hear that noise?' I asked as we rounded the corner. 'That was her chin hitting the ground.' We laughed.

Udaivilas was an amazing place. I don't think I had ever seen so much marble—black and white checked marble everywhere. So much so, that it almost played tricks on my eyes. We made our way to the gallery that housed artworks by prominent artists from all over the world. I found the Indian paintings very interesting, especially the modern abstracts.

'Should we go inside, Tarun?' I gestured to the hotel reception area.

'Why not. Would you like a drink?'

'Sounds good.' We walked over to the waiter. The couple from the hotel were waiting to be seated. I waved. She gave me one of those forced smiles and turned her back.

'Where can we have a drink?' I asked the waiter, as Tarun was a few paces behind me, checking a message on his phone.

'And will ma'am be drinking alone?' he said, looking me up and down, as Tarun came to stand right beside me. I was a bit taken aback with the waiter's question. Tarun, who had obviously been listening and watching, stepped forward and puffed out his chest. 'Ma'am will be drinking with me,' he said looking the waiter in the eye.

'I'll check,' he said picking up the phone, raised his nose in the air and looked about the lounge, which was almost empty.

'This way,' he pointed, and took us over to a dark corner of the lounge.

'What was that all about?' I asked as we took a seat. Tarun was not amused.

'He either thinks you picked me up or I picked you up and is being judgemental about it.'

'I should have told him you were my brother.' He laughed.

Just then his phone rang. He spoke in Hindi.

'Should we go somewhere else?' I asked once he was off the phone.

'All the family is at a friend's house on the other side of town. They would like us to come there.'

'That sounds wonderful.'

We never really spoke about it again, but on that first day of being brother and sister, we had come up against prejudices from both sides of our cultures. Somehow it bonded us even more.

'I'd rather be with your family anyway,' I told him as we took off again.

We were given a warm welcome when we arrived. All the children were busy playing and colouring in on the floor and Manisha and Poonam were in the kitchen helping to prepare dinner. Mamma was sitting on the lounge, and I joined her. She didn't say, but I could tell that she knew of our pledge. As is tradition, as a guest, I was served first and ate with the men. I was never comfortable with this, but what could I do? The food was delicious. The tables were cleared and then I wondered where the women were.

'Where's Manisha and Poonam?'

'They're eating in the kitchen.' I got up and walked into the kitchen. There they were, sitting cross-legged on the floor eating their food. I sat on the floor with them. At first, they looked surprised, but then gave me a broad smile as Manisha patted the floor, urging me to move in closer. 'Where did you get your kurta?' Poonam asked feeling the cloth. 'Is it silk?'

'Yes, I got it at Fabindia in Delhi, and the trousers as well.'

'I like it.'

'Very pretty,' Manisha added. 'Pink suits you, Barbie.'

'Very Indian,' Poonam gave Manisha a little wink. 'All she needs is henna. You like this?' Poonam held out her hand.

'I love henna.'

I was family now.

After dinner, the men sat and discussed 'men's business' and the women retreated to the bedroom and relaxed and chatted. I joined them. I had admired the henna on Poonam's hand, and so they then decided that I should get the full treatment. Poonam firstly prepared my hands with clove oil, and began an intricate pattern on my hand. We were seated on the corner of the bed. Mamma was a bit tired so lay down on the bed and had a nap beside us. All formalities had been lifted. Once Poonam had finished my henna, she squeezed lemon juice over the design to help set it, and then came and sat down beside me on the bed with Manisha. It was a cosy group and I felt a closeness that I hadn't felt before.

Earlier in the day, I knew that Raksha Bandhan, the brother–sister pledge, was important and not just a flippant gesture, but when I got back to my haveli, it dawned on me the enormity of the promise that Tarun had made to me; not only had I become his sister, but I had been accepted into his family. From that day on, when I visited the family house, we all sat at the table together for meals. I was family…I was no longer a tourist—a privilege I always treasure.

Terror, 2008

On 26 November 2008, India was brought to her knees when ten members of an Islamic militant organisation based in Pakistan, carried out a series of bombings and shootings in Mumbai. I watched in horror as scenes of the tragedy were broadcast globally on television. The attacks began that Wednesday evening, and continued on until the following Saturday morning. Nobody was safe. The attacks happened within minutes of each other at luxury hotels, a restaurant, the railway station, and even a hospital.

I cried. What was happening to my dear India? I felt sick in my stomach. A few months earlier, there had been bomb blasts in Jaipur, followed by Delhi, Bangalore and Ahmedabad. I prayed to keep Udaipur safe.

Even before the Mumbai attack, family and friends had been telling me, 'You won't be going back to India for a while.' I knew it was true. I was sad. I was angry.

I thought of Tarun and his family and wanted to call him, but communications were down. Graphic pictures continued to shock the world for several days. People were being systematically hunted down in their hotel rooms and shot. I wept. I wept for the families affected—some 164 people killed and over 300 wounded. I also wept for my Indian family. I wondered if life in India would ever be the same again.I recalled Tarun's voice when he had called some months earlier; he couldn't disguise his excitement.

'We've bought a block of land. We're going to build an eco resort.'

'Where's the land?'

'It is near Eklingi Temple. Remember, we went there.' His voice was proud and I could imagine his face as well. I could see his smile…those perfect white teeth. 'I'll send photos. You can help me in decorating.' An email arrived shortly after:

Hello dear sister,

How are you?

I'm sending some photo of land so I hope you will enjoy and give me good blessing for success because it will be really a big project for me but I will try.

Everybody is happy in my family.

Rudrakshi is going well.

Thanks, Tarun

It was a huge undertaking for the whole family. The photos showed desolate, rocky, barren ground with a splash of pink on the distant hills as Mamma surveyed the scene with Shakti by her side. Her profile on the edge of the escarpment, with the scarf of her sari blowing in the breeze, was quite regal. Manisha stood in the foreground in soft yellow, adding coolness to the harsh desert vegetation. She was standing side on. Could she be pregnant? I dared not ask. Maybe her sari had simply caught the wind.

I replied:

Land looks good. Thanks for photos. I send you many good blessings and you'll do a wonderful job. Everyone looks well. Busy here getting house ready for sale. Are the tourists still coming?

I'm still hoping to come this year—hoping for Diwali again, but have to see what happens here with the house. Fingers crossed. Do you have that saying in India? Let you know soon.

Love to all, Barbie

We were in the process of trying to sell our house in Sydney and of course could not make any definite plans. I sent photos of how I had decorated the house, and our guest bedroom with all my Indian bits and pieces.

He replied:

Hi Barbie, it's a heaven bedroom. You have nicely decorated. I love this really.

I'm sending u some photo so u can enjoy. One is my bike which I bought now n I love this bike. Also photo of Manisha in traditional dress.

Everybody love u n miss u very much.

Hope see u soon. Enjoy. Tarun.

I was so happy that he was now writing emails. He had not been confident with his written English, but the more he wrote, the more it improved. We also skyped and the whole family joined in. Even my big cat Max's image travelled to India, as they looked in amazement at every one of his 12 kilos.

Things dragged on with the house and it was obvious I wasn't going to visit for a while.

Hi Barbie, I hope maybe you may be coming in April and then if you will have time we can make our programme to go to KASHMIR yes why not...cross finger.

Ok see u soon I hope

Tarun.

As it was, Bob was worried about me going to India after the bomb blasts in Delhi, Jaipur and Bangalore and I have to say it made me nervous as well. Kashmir was also out of the question. The country was in a state of unrest. Thousands of youths had pelted security forces with rocks, burnt government buildings and attacked railway stations. Even if I crossed all my fingers and toes, I knew I would not be going to Kashmir with Tarun.

I read all the Indian newspapers online: *The Times of India, The Indian Express* and even the translated version of *The Hindi Times*. I was hungry for news; a glimmer of hope. It seemed that the latest bombings in Mumbai would leave India off the map for some time. No one was safe from these terrorists. The world had gone mad. I was devastated. Warnings were issued about the dangers of travelling to India. It would be almost two years before I returned.

Holi, 2010

'Come for Holi,' Tarun wrote to me. 'It'll be fun.'

Known as the Festival of Colour, Holi is one of the major festivals in India. It is held on the full moon day of February/March, celebrating the passing of winter, and the arrival of spring.

So, in February 2010, having not been to India in almost two years, I was more than eager as I set off for my first Holi experience.

'When do you arrive? Family is waiting,' Tarun texted me.

It was definitely time to go back. India stirred emotions in me that I found difficult to explain to myself, let alone anyone else, plus I had missed my Indian family.

My journey took me from Jaipur to Udaipur via Pushkar. I had decided I wanted to see more of the countryside, and had organised a driver and car to meet me in Jaipur. He was a jovial fellow, and during our trip, he shared at great length, the story of his life, his wife and children. At times, I struggled to stay awake. Then, as if trying to stir some interest from me, he said, 'I also have girlfriend in UK. She comes to India once a year and takes me on holidays.' He paused, waiting for a response.

'We stay at the best hotels,' he told me quite proudly. 'I pick her up at the airport and off we go.' Our eyes met in the rear-vision mirror. He was gauging my reaction. I said nothing. I wasn't there to judge him but I found it weird that he would want to share such a secret with a complete stranger. He obviously just needed to tell someone. 'And how about you?' he asked. 'Are you married?'

'Yes,' I replied promptly.

'Very good,' he said as he searched once more for my eyes in the mirror.

'I have a son around your age,' I told him. His eyes immediately flashed back to the mirror. I could almost hear his mind ticking over. He turned the radio on.

'Okay, so we will be in Pushkar soon.' His voice became more businesslike.

Pushkar had held an interest for me for some time, being one of the major holy sites in India. Pilgrims came from all over the subcontinent to take puja (an act of worship) in its famous lake, which boasts some 52 ghats. The city has hundreds of temples and is also famous for the Pushkar Camel Fair. It is held every October/November at the time of the full moon. Pushkar is surrounded by hills on three sides and the sands of the Thar Desert on the other, and it is from those sand dunes that camel traders, herders and horsemen arrive for the sales.

'Unfortunately, the lake is empty. They tried to clean the silt from the bottom,' my driver-turned-tour guide explained, 'and the water all disappeared in the sand.' It was disappointing to see, as apparently it had been full for 150 years. 'Now they wait for next monsoon,' he added.

I remembered how I felt on my first trip to Udaipur in 2005, when I found the lake there was dry. It seemed as if the soul of the city had been drained away. Water was the life of these desert cities. That was the year I met Tarun. I could never have imagined then how my trips to India would continue.

I spent my night in Pushkar at a little haveli called Dia, meaning 'a ray of light', on the outskirts of the city. It was peaceful and I was thankful for a rest after a day in the car with my chatty driver. It's sister haveli, Inn Seventh Heaven, was in the city and a shuttle bus ran between the two. The rooms were spacious and light with white muslin curtains gently caught the afternoon breeze. I poured myself a gin and tonic and lounged on a daybed on my balcony that looked out to the nearby hills with a temple at the very top. It seemed to me as if one's religious devotion was challenged as not only did you need to go to the temple daily, but the climb was incredibly steep. As I looked down on the dusty road below, a woman was guiding her goats to a field across the road. It was quiet; peaceful. I moved to the rooftop for sunset and watched as the fiery ball of light sunk below the horizon behind the temple, the sky left pink until the light faded.

Next morning, we were on the road around ten.

'We are waiting for you,' Tarun texted. 'When are you coming?'

'See you around 3 pm,' I replied. It was a long, hot journey to Udaipur. This time, I had booked a couple of days at Amet Haveli. I had watched it grow as renovations saw it blossom from a small haveli to a second level together with courtyard pool. It was originally built at the same time as the Palace on the Lake, and designed by the same architect. The owner was a friend of Tarun and Shakti, and had kindly shown me through the premises the very first time I visited.

As we neared Udaipur, I felt the same old butterflies in my tummy, and couldn't stop myself from smiling. I ticked off all the familiar landmarks as we drove into the old city. Tarun's friend Naresh was standing outside his leather shop. I waved. 'Barbie,' he called and waved back with a huge smile.

'These streets are so narrow,' the driver complained as he manoeuvred around a cow that had laid down in the middle of the road. The traffic came to a bottleneck at the top of the Old Palace Road.

'Not far now.' I did my best to pacify him.

'Where are you?' Tarun texted me. I had sent him a message when we were on the outskirts of town. 'Be there soon. Too much traffic,' I replied. We came to a standstill as we waited to cross the bridge across the backwaters of the lake. 'Almost there,' I told the driver.

A pair of huge elephant gates fortified with huge metal spikes stood at the entrance to Amet Haveli. In the past, those spikes were anything but decorative, and sent a stern warning to marauding enemies should they try to ram the gates using the strength of their elephants.

I looked for Tarun as we drove through. He was waiting in the courtyard. I saw him as we drove in and wound down the window and called to him. He waved and came over to the car. I had wondered if there would be any awkwardness between us after two years. There was none. We hugged. It was so good to see him. 'How are you, my sister?'

'I'm well, my brother.' We both laughed. 'It's been too long.'

I'd booked a room overlooking the lake. Once shown to my room, I went directly to the window seat and felt like a princess as I gazed directly onto the lake. A boat quietly motored by and its wash gently rose and fell wistfully against the outer wall of my room.

'Chai?' Tarun asked once my bags were delivered.

'Of course.'

We walked across to the Ambrai restaurant, within the grounds. The same waiter who had often served my breakfast on previous trips attended our table.

'Namaste,' he smiled in recognition. Seated under the mango tree, we gazed across to the palace on the lake.

'Happy?' Tarun asked as I leaned back in my seat and closed my eyes momentarily.

'So happy.' There was a splash as some young boys dived from the ghats. A woman sat on the stairs doing her laundry and used her hand to move the murky green moss on the edge away from her clothes. Across the lake, I could see the welcoming red carpet on the steps at the entrance to the Lake Palace. Workmen were busy white-washing the water stained walls that had risen from the depths as the water levels dropped.

'Family are waiting to see you,' he said after a while. 'Would you like to come to the house tonight?'

'Yes, I'm looking forward to seeing everyone, and most importantly, I'm anxious to meet your young son.'

Manisha had given birth to a boy the previous December. I remember the conversation when Tarun called to tell me.

'I have a son.' His voice was elated, his pride, obvious.

'What's his name?' I'd asked.

'So far, he has no name, but his name will start with the letter M. We can't decide.'

'Maybe you can call him Maharaja,' I said without thinking. It had been the first M name that came into my head.

'Okay. He will be Maharaja…Little Maharaja.' And so, he was known. I had named his child. It gave me an overwhelming feeling of love and connection to have been included in such an important family decision. His name remained so until he began school, and then he took his registered name of Rudraveer.

Now that I was in Udaipur, I felt I could relax. We sat a little longer finishing our chai. 'I will collect you around 7 o'clock,' he said with a cheeky smile. 'I have a surprise for you.'

'What is it?'

'You will have to wait and see. Big surprise.'

'Tell me.'

'Then it will not be a surprise.' He laughed. Like a typical brother, he enjoyed teasing me.

I went to my room and unpacked a few presents ready to take in the evening, and had a rest. I tried to think of what his surprise might be, but had no idea.

Around 7 pm, I went to the courtyard to wait for him. I was looking out for his white van or motorbike.

'Surprise!' I heard his voice as a left-hand drive army jeep came through the gates. He had a smile on his face a mile long. 'You like?' He jumped out effortlessly. The roof was off. It looked very smart. 'Let's go.'

I jumped in the front seat. It was wider than a normal car, especially the cars in Udaipur.

'I've only had it for six days,' he told me. All eyes were on us as he honked the horn to round yet another blind corner. Smaller cars moved to the side of the narrow streets to allow us through. Of course, there were no seatbelts, and I was sitting on the right-hand side, appearing as if I was driving.

I wanted to say 'slow down'. We seemed to be going quite fast.

'I'll take you to see the night view of the lake, and then we'll go to my house.' The night air was cool as it rushed through my hair, a welcome relief after the afternoon heat. The Monsoon Palace hung in a perfect night sky as if floating.

'It's good?' There was no wiping the smile off his face.

'It's great.'

'I love it.' I could tell.

We made our way to his family home. Further out, the road became less busy, and I was able to relax and take in the atmosphere. He tooted the horn on our arrival and everyone came out. Mamma was in all smiles. A few months ago, she had fallen, and after hospitalisation had to rest in bed for 45 days. But when she grabbed my hand and hugged me, her grip was strong. Mahipal was next out with big hugs, and then Riya and Rudrakshi.

'Hello Daddy.' Rudrakshi ran up to him. Manisha and Poonam greeted us just inside the door with some nibbles for the table. Little Maharaja was still awake and full of smiles— so cute. Kohl outlined his eyes. It seemed strange for a little boy, but that is their custom, to ward off the evil eye. He was their little prince.

'Do you like the jeep?' Rudrakshi asked me in perfect English. 'It's so much fun,' she answered before I could reply.

'I love it,' I told her. 'How is school?' It was amazing what a difference the time apart had made. They were all taller, more grown-up and even Manisha and Poonam spoke English. Mamma may have understood some, but didn't speak any.

'You will be here for Holi?' Riya asked, her eyes wide as she clapped her hands together.

'Holi is such fun,' Rudrakshi joined in. 'My favourite colour is pink. Do you like pink, Barbie?'

'I love pink.'

'We will play Holi.'

I had noticed that decorations had already started to appear around the city, heralding this special occasion.

Dinner was delicious as usual. 'Who wants to come for a ride in the jeep?' Tarun asked as we got up to leave. Of course, the three children ran out the door to the vehicle. It was almost 11 pm and the streets were quiet. Rudrakshi sat on the very edge of the back seat. 'Hold on tight,' I warned her as we took off. There were five of us in what was typically a three-seater. Of course, in Australia, it would have been completely illegal, but it reminded me of the time when we would all pile into my grandfather's car when I was a child. There was my father driving, with one of us, usually my brother, in the front between my father and my grandfather, and my mother and grandmother and the other four kids in the back. It was the way we travelled 50 years ago before seatbelts.

After two nights at Amet Haveli, I moved across to Kankawa, on the other side of the lake.

'Welcome Barbara,' Janardan greeted me. 'I have changed your room since last time you were here.' He showed me up the stairs. 'You now have your own private balcony overlooking the lake. What do you think?'

I would be able to sit out there anytime and leave my door open without any worry about other guests coming in. 'It's wonderful, Janardan.' There were two cane chairs and a table by the edge.

Once settled, I walked up to meet Tarun at Spicebox. He was taking me to see his new jewellery shop on the other side of the town. As well as Holi, it was also the start of a Muslim festival and the roads were being closed off to tuktuks and cars.

'We'll go on the bike,' he told me as I arrived. I no longer felt uncomfortable being his passenger. In fact, it was quite exhilarating.

The shop was in the foyer of a new hotel in the Lake Fateh Sagar region, some distance away. He had set it up very attractively, and was in a good position for tourists. I carefully examined all the jewellery, and then the hotel owner called in wanting to have a meeting with him. 'If you want to go back, best you go soon,' he said. 'Soon the tuktuks will not be allowed to come through and I might be a while here.'

I walked out onto the road, but there was not a tuktuk in sight. I tried to wave a couple down, but they continued on. Suddenly, I heard a voice, 'Barbie.' It was Mahendra, a young man who often worked with Tarun. 'Where you going Barbie?'

'I'm trying to get back to Kankawa,' I told him.

'Jump on.' He moved forward in his seat. His scooter was tiny, with no power at all. It struggled with the two of us on board. We moved slowly. All other bikes were passing us by. A man on an expensive, huge motorbike pulled up alongside and chatted to Mahendra in Hindi. His hair was slicked back and he wore sunglasses. We stopped. He stopped.

'Go with him,' Mahendra told me. 'He is going near to your hotel.'

I ungraciously dismounted and climbed on behind this unknown man. Mahendra waited while I got on.

I grabbed a hold of the two handles behind me on either side of the new bike. Whether for Mahendra's benefit or mine, he took off at great speed and then braked suddenly, thrusting my body forward against his, as a skinny dog ran out in front of us. I felt my boobs hit his back. Embarrassed, I straightened myself in my seat. His bike was fast and it was a wild ride back to the hotel amidst the traffic. I felt my knuckles going numb as I held myself taut so as not to brush against him each time he accelerated.

'Watch your leg,' he told me as a shiny red bike with gleaming chrome exhaust pipes pulled up beside us. I pulled me legs in tighter.

'Where you stay?' he asked. I thought he knew.

'Kankawa,' I told him.

'Okay, I know'. At the next stop in traffic, he reached into his pocket. 'Here is my card.' I put the card in my pocket without looking at it. He took off with another roar, passing all the smaller bikes along the way and pulled up outside Kankawa at the same speed. I held his shoulder as I got off.

'Balaji is my name,' he told me and extended his hand.

'Barbara.' I shook his hand. 'Thank you, Balaji.'

'Are you travelling alone?' he asked.

'I have friends here.'

'There is a party on Monday on my rooftop. Please come.'

'I'll tell my friend Tarun. Maybe, you know him.' And with that he revved his bike and disappeared. I turned around to find the local market boys watching me.

I brushed the hair out of my face and straightened by blouse. My legs wobbled as I climbed the stairs to my room. I was in need of a gin and tonic. What a whirlwind ride that had been. I poured my drink and retired to the cane chair to watch the sunset.

In the evening, Tarun and Shakti joined me at Kankawa for dinner.

'Do you know Balaji from the hotel up the street?' I asked Tarun.

'Do you mean Balaji with the big new motorbike?' he asked as he looked across to Shakti.

'Yes. He gave me a lift on his bike this afternoon.'

'Really.' My protective Indian brother leaned closer. 'How was it?'

'Scary,' I answered, and they both laughed

'He likes to impress,' Shakti added nodding his head. Tarun nodded in agreement.

'So,' he changed the subject, 'are you ready for Holi?'

'Tell me what happens?'

'Tomorrow night, there will be a special night at the City Palace. The Maharana and his family will attend. Some members of the public can go, but you need a ticket.'

'Where would I get a ticket?'

'Tomorrow, I will check with a friend who has contacts at the palace. We will see.'

In the morning, he picked me up in his van, and we headed towards the palace. We asked at the gate, and the official phoned through to the palace. The answer was no. Tarun called his friend. 'He is a good friend of the prince,' he told me as he waited for an answer. We were driving back down from the palace when he spotted his friend walking. He signalled to him and next minute he was in the van.

'What can I do to help?' his friend asked me. Oh, my goodness. I thought fast.

'I am writing a book about Udaipur and would like to include the festivals in my research. Of course, I would wish to portray them in the correct manner, and would love to attend the Holi festival at the palace tonight.'

'Come with me now,' he told me. 'We will go to the palace now and arrange.' I was flabbergasted, and looked down at my crushed blouse and rubber thongs.

'Now? I'm not terribly well prepared for the palace.'

'No matter. Come now.'

Tarun turned the van around and we were on our way back up to the palace. A wave of his friend's hand and we were through security. 'Follow me.' He opened the door of the van and walked ahead.

We passed more security guards, climbed some stairs to an office within the palace, and he introduced me to the event organiser. I was almost out of breath.

After hearing my story, he looked on his computer screen. 'I am sorry but all passes for journalists and the like have been given out. If you wish, I can organise a paid ticket for you.'

'How much would that be?'

It was around $A100. 'Can I possibly buy two?,' I asked. 'A local businessman would accompany me.'

'Let me see. Yes, yours is the last tourist ticket. You can buy one for local use.' I pulled the money from my bag and paid before he could change his mind. The tickets included drinks and dinner at the palace.

Tarun had waited in the van. 'I have to leave you here,' his friend shook my hand. 'Nice to meet you.'

'Thank you so much,' I said as I made my way back down to the van.

'Guess what?' I jumped back into the van.

'You have a ticket?' Tarun asked.

'Surprise brother. I have two tickets. We are going to the palace tonight.'

I wish I had taken a photo of the look on his face. His eyes opened wide in disbelief. He sat for a moment taking in what I had said.

'Really!'

'Yes really.'

'The palace? Me?'

I saw his mind ticking over. 'I need to go and have a haircut,' he said seriously and then laughed. 'The palace!'

He dropped me off to Kankawa. 'I need to get my suit out,' he said as he left, 'and polish my shoes,' he called out the window. I hadn't worked out what I was going to wear there.

'Wear that red outfit you got for the wedding,' he called back to me. 'We'll go in the jeep.'

As I walked back to my room, it dawned on me that he had lived all his life in Udaipur, but of course, would never have paid that amount for a night of entertainment at the palace. It was my gift to him for all the things he had done for me. I have to say, I was also very excited.

By that stage, it was just after midday, and he would collect me around 4:00 pm. I pulled my red sari top out of my bag along with my beige silk pants. The pants were crumpled. I dashed out to the local ironing man, who operated out of nothing more than a hole in the wall. I washed my hair and picked out some jewellery to wear for this special occasion.

By 3:50 pm, I was waiting in the courtyard. 'You look like you are certainly going somewhere special,' Janardan commented.

'The City Palace for Holi.'

'Say hi to the Maharana for me,' he laughed.

Tarun arrived in the jeep. He was wearing a dark suit and white shirt with a red silk scarf and matching piece in his pocket. He looked very handsome.

'You are looking very good,' he said. 'Let's go to the palace.' He climbed carefully into his seat and sat tall, his head held high. He drove up through the palace gates and was given the all clear by security. We parked, and then walked to the seating area to view the Maharana's entrance. I could see that his chest was puffed out. He had never been to anything so grand.

We were shown to our seats overlooking the lawn, where deep blue carpet and white lounge chairs had been laid out for the dignitaries.

'Where do they get all the flowers?' I asked. Water fountains were decorated with the petals of roses, marigolds and sweet jasmine. It was like nothing I had ever seen before. Tarun was beside himself. 'Thank you,' he said over and over. 'I will always remember this.'

We had arrived early and were able to watch the spectacle unfolding. The men looked resplendent in their white suits with colourful turbans. The colours for Holi for women are red and white, and everywhere the saris sparkled. You can never overdress in India.

A trumpet blast from a tower high in the palace brought everyone to attention. Two marching bands in full military colours heralded the arrival of royalty. The Maharani arrived with her daughters, followed by her son, the Prince in cream with a pink turban and maroon shoes. They took their seats in the front row on a comfortable lounge.

Two riders on white horses led the Maharana's carriage through the gates. His youngest granddaughter of around six years sat beside him. Her eyes darted around as photographers flashed their cameras at her, and she watched as the band stood to attention at their arrival. Silver-leafed seats with red and orange silk cushions awaited the Maharana and his family. In the centre of the courtyard was a huge unlit bonfire some 10 metres tall. It was encircled by a border of rose and marigold petals. The press was there in force. A huge camera swung from a trapeze and searched the crowd. 'They're filming you,' Tarun nudged me as it flew past us. We laughed, enjoying our moment with royalty.

The sun was beginning to set, and the palace was strung with fairy lights from one end to the other. I looked up and saw monkeys up in the tower above. They had the best seat. I wondered what they thought.

The Maharana took his granddaughter by the hand and led her to the huge bonfire. They circled it in what was obviously a tradition. A stick of fire was brought to him and he lit the pile of branches. Flames reached high and illuminated the whole of the palace. A barefoot group danced around the fire to the beat of drums, and I felt for them as bits of ash and flame blew from the fire into their path.

Once this was over, we were led to another courtyard, where tables were set for dinner. Festoons of flowers, along with fairy lights hung from large umbrellas above each table. Only in India, could they do something as spectacular. We were seated with guests from the Lake Palace. Drinks were served.

'Red wine please,' Tarun had settled in and was enjoying the attention. He had a permanent smile on his face. Waiters served the very best of food, and then we were able to have our photo taken with both the Maharana and the Prince. Tarun was proud.

'That was amazing,' he told me on the way back to the jeep.

'I'm so glad I was able to share that with you.'

As we drove out of the palace and onto the palace road, Tarun stopped. The whole family was waiting for us beside the lake. He must have texted them as we were leaving. They wanted to know every detail.

'How was it? Did you see the Maharana? Did you see the Prince? 'There were lots of questions. What a night! To have them waiting for us was so special.

'See you early tomorrow,' Shakti told me. 'Tomorrow is Festival of Colour. Be ready.'

'I'll be ready.'

Later, as I got into bed, I was still on a high. I pinched myself. Had I really been to the palace? Had I met the Maharana? I looked at the photos I had taken. Yes, I had. That was me standing beside him. I lay there for ages reliving every moment before I dozed off.

There was no sleeping-in the next morning, as fireworks had gone off continually all night. I was on the rooftop having breakfast when I received a text from Tarun. 'Come, play Holi. We are at Spicebox.' I quickly finished my chai and walked up the street. I had put on my older white clothes as I had been warned not to wear anything special. As it was, I had been showered with pink in my hair on the way out by Janardan. Even Bambi, the German Shepherd had a touch of pink and green on her coat. On the road outside Spicebox, I could see Tarun, Shakti, Mahipal, Riya and Rudrakshi. The games had already begun, and they were waiting for me. 'Happy Holi,' Tarun greeted me and wiped my cheeks with hot pink. They had bags of colour, and I was quick to join in. There was no running away, it was inevitable. My face was covered in pink, green, yellow and purple. Shakti had beautiful yellow hair and red face, while Mahipal had a green face. Rudrakshi screamed while her face was covered in yellow powder. Further down the street, there were clouds of colour. The next thing to follow the colour, was water… water pistols, buckets of water. People were throwing both colour and water from the windows above. There was no escaping it.

We all piled into the jeep and headed to Tarun's uncle's place. I was sitting in the front, and I saw a young boy ahead with one of those soaker water pistols. I watched him load it with water from the drain, and then as we came closer, he aimed it straight at my face. I was soaked. It went up my nose, in my mouth and all over me. In the jeep, I was a sitting target, and my blonde hair would have been a beacon. The streets were full of people throwing colour and water. It was quite chaotic. My clothes never came clean. Originally, I was told, the colour was made from vegetable dyes, the pink from pomegranates, but now it was all commercially produced.

I was leaving for home that night. My hair was still pink but that didn't worry me. I must have looked a sight with my hennaed hands and my coloured hair.

The whole family took me to the airport again. I loved them all and it was sad to leave. 'I'll be back soon,' I waved. I fell sick as soon as I got back home. It was thought I had ingested a germ when I was hit by the water blaster. When you think about it—those drains from where he filled his pistol would be an outlet for all household waste as well as rats and their droppings.

I was alone at home, and did not know what to do. Bob was in Sydney. I was up all night with vomiting and diarrhoea, barely managing to drag myself to the bathroom. I wasn't sure whether to call someone, an ambulance or what. By morning, I was very weak and drove myself to the hospital where I was immediately put on a drip for the day. I slept there all day. I can honestly say that it was the sickest I have ever been after an India trip. It would not put me off going back though, but it took a little time to recover.

Hotel Pratap Bhawan, 2011

I had always felt that my travels in India would not be complete without a visit to the Taj Lake Palace, commonly known as the Lake Palace in Udaipur. For me, it encapsulated the history and romance of India, and having been built by a maharana as a present for his wife only added to the fascination.

Since my first trip, I had witnessed it sitting high and dry during a drought, most likely looking very much as it did when it was originally built, and before the monsoon rains had been channelled to fill the lake. I had written about it, painted it, and spent most of my time in Udaipur sitting and gazing at it. I decided to write to the palace before my arrival and ask for an appointment. Previously, it had been possible to go there for dinner, but with terror attacks, security had been tightened and entry would only be allowed to paying guests.

'What do you think my chances are?' I had asked Tarun, while we were Skyping. I had sent an email to the palace with an image of a mock-up cover for my book. It was a photo of me taken from the rooftop of Kankawa with the Lake Palace in the background.

'We will keep fingers crossed for you.' I had received no reply from the palace before I left Australia.

'I've booked you into a very good hotel in Udaipur,' he laughed.

'Why are you laughing?' I could tell that he was up to something.

'We have bought a hotel. Can you believe?'

'And I'm going to stay there?'

'Yes, of course. Your room is ready.'

'That's huge, Tarun.'

I remembered our conversation just the year before when I asked him about his dream for the future.

'You have Spicebox, the jewellery shops…what's next?' He thought for only a few moments.

'Truly, my dream would be to own a hotel. Yes, that is my dream. You can help me decorate it.'

I admired his confidence, his determination. He would make up his mind about something, and go after it.

'There is a place I would like in the future,' he had told me. 'It is not for sale at moment.'

'Where is it?'

'We can walk. It's close by.' As we walked down the street, Tarun pointed out a lovely old heritage building standing on the corner. Its entry was set above street level with two imposing front doors. It was painted white.

'What do you think? It has nine guest rooms and the rooftop overlooks the lake.'

'I can imagine you there,' I'd told him.

So, one year later, he had managed to take his dream and turn it into a reality. The old man who owned the hotel, had retired and sold up. Tarun never ceased to amaze me.

It was hard to believe that 12 months had passed since that visit. I was so looking forward to seeing everyone again and had bought some duty-free whisky for Tarun and perfume for Manisha, Poonam and Mamma before taking my seat at the gate lounge. My flight would arrive in Delhi around 10 pm and I would stay there the night. I had never spent much time in Delhi. I guess I hadn't gotten to know it and didn't really feel confident by myself in such a huge city. The traffic was horrendous and I had no real sense of direction. I had found accommodation at the Krishna Hotel, centrally located and felt quite comfortable there. Next morning, I'd catch a train to Jaipur, and then a car to Udaipur. Tarun had made the bookings for me. It would be my first train trip on my own, and I was a little nervous. The five-hour trip cost 550 rupees, which was around $A12. I was wondering what sort of seat I would be getting for that price, as it also included breakfast and morning tea.

My phone beeped just as I arrived in my Delhi hotel. 'Welcome to India, sister,' the message read. 'See you tomorrow.'

Train departure time next morning was 6:20 am and it was still dark when I left the Krishna Hotel in a tuktuk. Sleep had been brief. Luckily, I arrived at the station early, as the train left ten minutes before scheduled time. India was full of surprises like that. I needed to catch my breath after running to keep up with the young man who carried my baggage to my carriage.

He dropped my bags and held out his hand. 'Four hundred rupees,' he said. I offered 200. After all, my five-hour train trip was only costing 550 rupees. He stood over me until I relented. I'm not good with confrontation with a carriage full of people watching.

My seat was by the window, beside an elderly man who was travelling with his wife. Once the train was in motion, we were given a small tray called a 'tea kit' comprising of two tea bags, two sugars and a creamer, together with two butterscotch lollies and a small packet of biscuits. A thermos of hot water and a cup had followed.

It was a foggy morning, and the stark silhouettes of the kesari trees disappeared into the mist as the train tracks raced along below my window, the early morning light reflecting off the rubbish strewn on the ground. The carriage was more dusty than dirty, but not as bad as I had imagined for such a cheap price. I felt like I was looking through dirty glasses, and there was a temptation to get out my hand wipes and clean my window, but I resisted, realising it was dirty on the outside as well. The old man next to me spoke no English but was keen to communicate. I showed him a photo of where I was going. He nodded. I also showed him a photo of where I was from. More nodding.

It was an express train and did not slow down as we powered through station after station. On the platforms, people stood shrouded in the fog like statues, awaiting their trains. Daylight began to appear, and the soft red of the earth became visible as I travelled backwards towards Jaipur.

The old guy read the newspaper. His left elbow had claimed our shared armrest leaving me squashed up against the window. Ghostly images of old buildings with peeling paint drifted by in the fog.

As we passed through another town, a young boy ran beside the train, matching his stride with the spacing of the railway sleepers. In the early morning light, I could see the faces of the villagers as they crouched beside the tracks, trousers down, performing their morning bodily motions. They were not perturbed by the passing of the train, and stared back. Some even waved. I thought of the movie *Slumdog Millionaire*, with similar images.

We were passing through Alwar. I had seen the sign, and actually found a spot on the window where it was a little cleaner, and tried to take a video. My camera intrigued the old boy.

Another cup of tea arrived. The old man was pulling hairs out of his nose as he tried to make conversation. Please, no! I looked again and he was still picking. He examined each hair, and then, yuk, he flicked it onto the back of the seat in front. His wife had gone to sleep. There had been heaps of room on her side, but he leaned towards me. I would have moved but the train was full. I diverted my eyes to the dirty window and a line of women carrying water vessels passed by. My phone beeped, attracting the old man's attention.

It was a text message from Tarun. 'How is train?' I could sense the old man peering over my shoulder as I read it.

What could I say? 'Train's good. I'll call you when I get to Jaipur.'

Breakfast was served. It was vegetable curry with rice and chapatti, together with chutney and yoghurt. Much more than I expected. The old man straightened up in his seat to eat, allowing me to do the same. I had noticed earlier, at quite close range, that he was missing most of his teeth. I could hear his gummy lips smacking together as he ate. I giggled to myself. He made himself another cup of tea from the thermos and proceeded to dunk his remaining biscuits, retrieved them at the last moment and then leaned forward, opened his mouth wide, and took them whole into his mouth. I tried to contain my smile as it rekindled a memory of my grandfather. He loved dunking biscuits. As a little girl, I would sit on his lap and dunk them for him. Sometimes, we would go through half a packet of gingernuts or Arnott's Milk Arrowroot before my grandmother would whisk the packet away. I hadn't thought of that in years.

We'd been travelling for three hours and the morning sunshine tried its best to filter through the dirty windows. After breakfast, the old man had laid his head back and dozed off. Travelling backwards was not my cup of tea. By the time I saw anything interesting, it had already passed and was lost in the distance.

The train arrived early and I wondered if my driver would be there. I saw the sign 'Bobera'. That's me, I thought.

'My name is Ajay,' he told me. 'I will take you to Udaipur.' He packed my bags into the boot. 'We should be there before dark.'

I made myself comfortable in the back seat. It had been an early start. I would probably sleep.

'Do you like music?' he asked.

'Yes.'

'Indian music?'

'Yes.'

'I always wanted to be a singer,' he told me. Sounded like I wouldn't be sleeping. He sang most of the way and I dozed off. By late afternoon, we were on the outskirts of Udaipur.

'Which hotel ma'am?' Ajay asked.

'Do you know Pratap Bhawan? Behind the temple? Lal Ghat? You know?'

'I know.'

I sent a message to Tarun. 'Almost there.' He was waiting at the top of the stairs when we arrived. His face lit up with the biggest smile. He stretched his arms out as I reached the top step. 'Welcome.' We hugged.

'Please come in. This is our hotel.' A young boy came down the spiral marble staircase. 'Dharma, this is Barbie. Please take her bags to her room… the one I showed you.'

'Namaste,' Dharma greeted me, bringing his hands together.

'Namaste.'

'What do you think? Do you like it?' His wide grin said it all.

'It's quite grand.'

The whole of the ground floor was a reception area with seating and coffee table to one side. The ceilings were high and a wide marble staircase led upstairs. 'I love it.'

'Come to the rooftop.' He led me up the stairs. 'There are nine rooms, four on each of the first two levels and one on the third floor.' I held the heavy timber handrail as we climbed up. 'Your room,' he pointed to number five and opened the door.

'What a large room.' There were twin beds, a dressing table, and table and chairs closer to the window and window seat. To the right was the bathroom. 'I can see why you liked it.'

'Now, from the rooftop you can see the lake and the palace.'

We climbed to the top level. It was just on sunset and the reflections of the disappearing sun illuminated a pink sky. On one side was the City Palace, so close you could almost reach over and touch it. Behind was the temple and I could hear the gentle repetitive chant of the call to prayer. Best of all, directly in front was the lake and the Lake Palace.

'We can go higher.' He pointed to more of a ladder than a staircase that led up to the water tanks. There was a table and some chairs up there.

'A good place for a gin and tonic,' he laughed.

'Would you like one? I brought some gin with me.'

'Okay, I will send Dharma for some tonic.' He used his phone.

The sun had gone down, and now all the fairytale lights began to come on.

'It's magic,' Tarun said taking in a deep breath. 'One day, we will have restaurant up here.' I could see his dream.

'Little by little,' he said. 'Slowly, slowly.' That was how he did things…slowly, slowly, but moving forward all the time. His mind was always thinking ahead.

'Dharma is bringing tonic and glasses.'

'I'll go and get the holy water from my room,' I said, and Tarun chuckled. I had been known to carry gin in a water bottle, and often ordered a lime juice with soda, and then casually added a splash of holy water. It was our joke.

We settled down with our drinks. 'There are small things we can do. We have painted inside. We need to paint the numbers outside each room. Could you do that while you are here?'

'Of course, just tell me what you would like me to do. I could do it in the traditional way with flowers like I've seen at other hotels.'

'Yes, that would be good.' I could see his mind ticking over.

'How are the family?'

'They are looking forward to seeing you. There are school exams tomorrow, so in the evening, you can come to the house for dinner. Tonight, we can eat at Ambrai. I will book.'

It was a quick meal. I was really tired after my early start and all the travelling. Once back, I was asleep in no time, but woke with pains in the tummy in the early hours. Here we go again. Was it something I had eaten on the train? I'll never know. It almost seemed like an initiation I had to go through each time I arrived in India, I thought to myself as I tossed and turned.

I phoned Tarun in the morning. 'Don't worry,' he said. 'I'll call the doctor. He's a friend of mine. He's also doctor to the Maharana. Rest and I'll let you know when he's coming.'

I dozed off. I had been awake since daylight and had watched the man on the nearby rooftop sweep the floor and set up the tables for breakfast. Around nine o'clock, there was a knock at the door. 'I have a cup of tea for you.' It was Tarun. 'How you feeling?'

'Lousy.' Oh no. 'Please excuse…' I jumped out of bed again and made a dash for the bathroom. I'd been throwing up most of the night. I was embarrassed that he would hear me. I had no choice. I composed myself and returned to my bed, wasted.

'Poor Barbie. Dharma is making some boiled rice for you. Best thing. Yes, boiled rice and banana are good for upset tummy.'

There was another knock. Tarun answered and it was his doctor friend.

'So, this is the patient. You have upset stomach?'

'Yes, pains, vomiting, diarrhoea. Everything.'

'We can fix.' He pressed my stomach, took my temperature and then wrote out a prescription. 'Take these. You will feel better by this afternoon. They will also make you sleep.'

Tarun sent Dharma off to the pharmacy. I took the pills and sleep took over. I didn't wake until around 4 pm, and felt much better. It went as quickly as it came. The sleep had helped.

I showered, washed my hair and put on my new white linen trousers and a cheery hot pink top and walked down the stairs.

'She's back.' Tarun clapped his hands. 'You look better.'

'I couldn't have looked any worse,' I laughed. 'Thank you for looking after me.' He gave his head that little half waggle.

'I think I'll go for a walk. Maybe I'll find some paint, and tomorrow I can start on the numbers.'

I remembered having seen an art school. They would know where to get paint. I also wanted to check my emails and there was an internet cafe nearby. On checking, there was an email from the Taj Lake Palace.

Dear Ms. Carmichael,
Greetings from Taj Lake Palace, Udaipur!

Please accept my apologies for the delay in getting back to you. Further to your mail, we are pleased to confirm your visit to the Lake Palace at a date convenient to you. Request you kindly advise on the same a day prior to arrival.

We look forward to meeting with you.

It was signed by the Sales Manager, Taj Lake Palace, Udaipur. I rushed back to the hotel to tell Tarun.

'I got an invite from the Lake Palace. Would you come with me?'

'Me?'

'Yes, you. We've been invited to morning tea.'

'I've never been inside.' He paused a moment. 'Once I delivered a parcel to the entrance, but never inside.'

'How about day after tomorrow? I'll call them.' He nodded excitedly.

The next morning, I was up early—a new person. I had breakfast and, armed with the paints and brushes I had bought, started the job. I felt at home at the hotel. There was a welcoming ambience to it. I began on my own room first, painting the number five in black, and then decorated with a traditional Indian floral design around it. It looked good. I was pleased.

'Very nice ma'am,' Dharma examined my work. 'You artist Ma'am?'

'Yes. You like?' He smiled.

By the time Tarun arrived I had finished the first two floors. He stood back and admired. 'It's perfect.'

On the rooftop, a seat was built into the wall. 'How about some decoration here?' I pointed to the pillars on either side.

'You are the decorator.'

He sat and watched while I painted the last flower. I could tell he was pleased.

'Do you have any plans this afternoon? My friend has an equestrian centre about an hour out of the city,' he told me. 'It's part of a small village. We could go after lunch.'

'Sounds good.'

'Okay, I'll pick you up at 1 pm.'

The Marigold Hotel, 2011

'My friend breeds horses,' Tarun told me as we set off on our afternoon journey. 'It's also a hotel where people come to ride horses.'

We took the highway for some time and then turned off onto a narrow country road. Cactus hedges fenced the fields. The countryside was so different to the other side of Udaipur, where the Aravalli mountain range semicircled the city.

Ravla Khempur, the hotel, was on the edge of the village. 'Ravla,' Tarun told me, 'is the Rajasthani name for the home of a chieftain.'

Tarun tooted his horn as we arrived and a man came out and opened the gates. We parked and walked towards the entrance. There was a sign—'The Best Exotic Marigold Hotel for the Elderly and the Beautiful'.

'Is this an old people's home?' I asked. Tarun looked confused. A little old man with a walking stick greeted us with a 'Namaste' as he walked by. Tarun looked at the sign again.

'There was no sign last time I was here,' he said. The building was like an old palace and by the look of it, was once painted pale yellow, but the walls were now stained and the paint peeling. Somehow, it still seemed to hold that romantic link to the past. It was a graceful old building. Bougainvillea burst out of old pots and stunted frangipanis sprouted flowers. I liked it. It had quite a welcoming ambience about it.

'This,' I thought to myself, 'is my idea of an authentic Rajasthani haveli. There was no turbaned man at the door to greet guests, no fancy reception, just a warm welcome.'

Tarun's friend, Mr Mahendra Singh came out to meet us. 'What is the sign for?' Tarun asked him before any introductions.

'They've been making a movie here. Welcome, please come in.' He led us across the courtyard and into a sitting room. 'Chai?' and with that he sent a young boy off to prepare. The room was quite dark. However, I could make out the many photographs and paintings of horses on the walls. He turned on some lights. An oversized rug covered the floor. Horse trophies adorned the shelves, along with books on horses.

'They have just finished filming here,' he continued. 'Many English actors.'

'Judi Dench was in Udaipur recently,' Tarun commented. 'They filmed at a hotel near us.'

'Yes, she was in movie,' his friend said. My ears pricked up.

'This is Barbie. She's from Australia. She loves India.'

'Would you like a little tour Barbie, while the chai is being made?'

We went back through the courtyard and up a flight of steep narrow steps that led to a covered veranda. Arched openings framed the view down to the stables where horses were being groomed. When we had driven in through the gate, I had pointed out a huge black horse. 'Look at his ears,' I had said to Tarun.

They're pointy towards each other. I've never seen a horse like that before. The horse had turned its head towards us. It was a magnificent creature, tall and strong.

'They're an old breed of Rajasthani horses,' he told me. 'They date back to the time of the Rajputs. They're Marwari horses.' The ones in the stables were the same breed.

The staircase continued up to the top level. There, only the facade remained. The view was across the village farms, and closer within the grounds, was a tiny temple.

The young boy appeared letting us know the chai was ready in the sitting room. Tarun and his friend conversed in Hindi and I walked around with my cup in hand, interested to see all the artefacts.

'Shall we take a walk to the stables?' his friend asked once we had finished. My nose twitched as I got a whiff of fresh hay and horse manure, followed by the scent of old leather saddles. These horses were the most outstanding I had ever seen; all had that regal look about them. Their pointed ears stood upright and almost made a heart shape.

'These horses are rarely seen now,' he told us. 'They were at a point of almost becoming extinct, but now people are breeding them again. Sometimes, you might see white ones being used for weddings.' I had seen wedding processions at times, where the groom, mounted on a decorated white horse, was led to his wedding ceremony. Often, a young boy would sit in front of him to bring good luck.

The same little old man came and walked beside us. I had my camera and he asked if I would like his photo. I took it as he flashed me a toothless smile, and then he wanted a photo with me. He was dressed all in white with a turban as well, and his oversized shoes flip-flopped as he walked. His dusty dhoti was tied exposing his thin, bandy legs, and his walking stick was fashioned out of an old tree branch. He waggled his head from side to side, quite proud of his own importance.

'There's been too many movie stars here,' laughed Tarun's friend. 'Now they all want their photos taken.'

Tarun took my camera and took photos of me with the old man, who held his head high and brushed the dust off his white clothing. At that stage, I had never heard of the Marigold Hotel or the movie. Once back at the hotel, I looked it up and followed it right to the time of its release in mid-2012. I bought the book *These Foolish Things* by Deborah Moggach, from which the screenplay was written.

Enticed by advertisements for a luxury retirement home in India, a group of strangers leave England to begin a new life. On arrival, however, they discover the palace is a shell of its former self, the staff are more than eccentric, and the days of the Raj appear to be long gone. But, as they soon discover, life and love can begin again, even in the most unexpected circumstances.

As I read, it seemed as though the book had been written with Ravla Khempur in mind, as each scene placed me in a different part of this majestic old building.

Two years later, when it came out, I would go to the movies with a friend in Byron Bay. There was a power cut midway through the movie and we were all evacuated. I laughed. 'It's just like being in India,' I told her. I would eventually end up seeing the entire movie, and it would become one of my favourites. It was much more special as I had seen Ravla Khempur come to life as the Marigold Hotel. I think the movie inspired many travellers, especially women, to travel to India.

I had known nothing of this on my first visit to Ravla Khempur. Once we had seen the stables, Tarun's friend directed us to the accommodation. 'I'd like to stay here one day,' I announced as we were shown over the bedrooms. They were quite basic, but comfortable with coloured glass windows sending beams of colour onto the walls. It would be a great place to just chill out and relax, I thought to myself—a good place to read a book or write one.

'It's very quiet here now, as the film crew have just left.' The place was deserted.

'Did the actors stay here?' I asked.

'No, they came by coach each day from Udaipur. They stayed at Udaivilas.' Udaivilas has a reputation of being one of the best hotels in the world.

'Luxury!' exclaimed Tarun.

We left in time to get back to Udaipur before dark.

'I'm looking forward to seeing that movie,' I told Tarun. 'Did you see any movie stars in Udaipur?'

'No, but my friend said that Judi Dench came into his shop.' He was very happy.

'Don't forget, tomorrow we are going to the Lake Palace.'

'Of course not.'

Out of the blue, Tarun started singing on the way home. He would often just burst into song. The first time he sang, I didn't know where to look. Our culture is so much more reserved. I'd never had anyone sing to me before, but singing and dancing is a natural part of his everyday life. He was never self-conscious. Now, knowing him as I did, I was able to enjoy it. He sang traditional Hindi songs that told a story. I couldn't translate, but the rich smooth tones of his voice reverberated in the car and made the journey back very pleasant.

The Taj Lake Palace Hotel, 2011

When we got back to the Pratap Bahwan that evening, Dharma was waiting for Tarun.

'Kalyan's wife is sick. He had to go back to the village,' he told him. Kalyan was the cook and that meant there would be no one to cook breakfast for the guests the next morning. Tarun looked troubled.

'I can cook breakfast,' I offered. The menu was quite simple—toast and eggs. Dharma's little eyes nearly popped out of his head.

'Are you sure?' Tarun asked.

'I'm sure.' I was quite excited at the prospect. 'Scrambled eggs, poached eggs, fried eggs, toast, porridge—easy. Not everyone comes down at once. It'll be fine.' We weren't going to the Palace until 11 am so there was heaps of time. 'Show me the kitchen now, so I know where everything is.'

The kitchen was very basic. There was a two-burner portable gas stove, two frypans, and a saucepan. Just like camping, I thought to myself.

'Is there a toaster?' I asked.

'No, we make the toast in the frypan. Dharma, you can help Barbie in the morning.'

'Okay.' Dharma nodded his head but I could tell he wasn't quite convinced.

'Is there a kettle?'

'No, we boil the water in the saucepan.' The saucepan had no handle and there was a pair of pliers to lift it on and off the gas burner. It was basic.

'I'll be down here at seven in the morning.'

I was happy that I was able to help.

When I came down the stairs in the morning, Dharma was waiting for me. 'You can cook ma'am?'

'Yes Dharma, I can.' I walked into the kitchen. 'First, we wash our hands.'

'Wash ma'am?' I grabbed the soap and lathered up my hands as I handed it to him.

'Okay, ma'am.'

There wasn't anyone waiting for breakfast. 'Do you know how to make chai, Dharma?' He nodded. 'Well, first you can make chai for you and me.' I always need a tea or coffee first up in the morning.

'I will get milk, ma'am.' He disappeared out of the door and returned with a container of milk. I don't know where he went as the shops were still closed.

I watched him fill the saucepan and light the gas burner. This afternoon I am taking Tarun shopping for a toaster and a kettle, I told myself. They hadn't been in the hotel very long and were still stocking it with the bare necessities.

My phone rang. It was Tarun. 'Are you sure you are okay with the breakfasts?'

'No problem.'

'Okay, see you at 10.'

Dharma came to the kitchen door. 'Room number 3 is here Ma'am for breakfast.'

'Give them menu Dharma and I will come.'

It was a couple from Melbourne. I explained the story about Kalyan. 'So, what would you like?'

'Scrambled eggs on toast for two, one tea and one coffee.'

'Too easy.'

Dharma follows me back to the kitchen. 'You make the tea and coffee,' I tell him, 'and then the toast. I'll do the eggs.' He smiled. He was enjoying it.

I beat the eggs and added some milk. 'Milk ma'am? Kalyan uses water.'

'I'm the cook today, Dharma.'

I looked over as he made the toast. He pressed the thin slices of bread down on the base of the frypan with his hand. At least they were clean. Yes, I was definitely buying a toaster today.

We had the breakfast out in no time. The eggs were nice and fluffy. The guests were happy. Dharma was happy and I was happy. We worked well as a team and everyone had gone by 9:30.

'I do dishes, ma'am.'

Great, that allowed me to go and get ready for my Cinderella trip to the Palace.

What should I wear? I hadn't come with a lot of good gear, but settled on my white linen pants and top. It looked fresh and I added a little jewellery. Tarun arrived in the jeep in nice shirt and jacket.

'Your carriage awaits,' he laughed as I stepped up into the front seat.

Our instructions were to go to the wharf in the grounds of the City Palace. There we would have to go through a security check. We were given the all clear. Next, we were directed to one of the palace's boats and given life jackets. The lake was beautiful that morning. The air was still and the lake was like glass, mirroring the palace's white walls. I looked back towards the city and the many havelis nestled on the lake's banks. I could pick out the room where I had stayed at Kankawa with its Lake Palace view. On the ghats below, women were doing their laundry and the washing hung on makeshift lines. Rooftop restaurants clamoured for the view, and their advertising paraphernalia for lunch and dinner were strung out for all to see. I looked back to the palace with its sparkling white walls, and could see two men in a boat touching up the soiled paintwork where the waterline had left its mark.

Back on the shore, the walls were streaked with dirty marks and peeling paint. I realised that the view from the shore towards the palace was the most spectacular one. I found it quite ironic that the cheap little room I had stayed in had a better view than that from the palace.

'I'm excited,' I told Tarun, as the boat edged into the pontoon.

'It's a very special day,' he said as he sat up straight and puffed out his chest.

A tall man in a red turban was waiting on the steps of the palace. He directed us to the main entry. As we approached the door, we were showered with rose petals. How beautiful. We were then shown to a table and chairs in the reception area and served a 'welcome drink'.

'I like this very much.' Tarun tried it. It was a mixture of fruit and spices—cool and refreshing.

From inside, looking out, it appeared as if we were on an island. If I hadn't seen firsthand when the lake was in drought, I would have wondered how this amazing place seemingly floated out there in the middle of the lake. Its foundations are set in the bed of the lake, and the palace was built first, and then the city was walled and the lake filled from the monsoons.

Immaculately-dressed staff flitted here and there attending to guests. Our host, Rachita, the hotel's Sales Manager came over and introduced herself.

'Welcome to the Taj Lake Palace.' She handed me a large envelope. 'This will give you information about the palace.' She sat down. 'Finish your refreshments and I will show you around. Tell me about your book.'

'It's a travel memoir based mostly in Udaipur,' I explained. 'The Lake Palace is the focal point of Udaipur, as well as being one of my favourite places in the world.'

'Come, and we'll walk around. We're almost fully booked, but I can show you one of our suites.' She led us up some stairs, and opened the door. It looked and felt how I would imagine the room of a princess to be. A grand four-poster bed was laid with extravagant cushions and bolsters in red and gold, and set into a scalloped arch in the wall. Above, the cornices and ceilings were elaborately decorated. Arched windows of red and green glass showered the room in colourful light. Hanging from the ceiling by ornate chains was a swinging seat, upholstered in red with bolsters at either end. A window seat the size of a large bed with plump cushions stacked high, looked out on the lake, the City Palace and the city itself. I don't think I had ever seen such opulence. I could have locked myself away in there forever, not wanting to be rescued.

Unfortunately for us, some lucky guest would be arriving soon, and this princess would have to leave her chambers. Neither Tarun nor I had said much, both taken aback by the sheer elaborateness. 'It's fit for a king,' he said at last.

Rachita led us back down to the courtyard. 'We have three restaurants here,' she told us. 'I have ordered morning tea for you. Take a seat and it will be brought to you.'

'Thank you.' We were not expecting such hospitality.

'Afterwards, feel free to wander around.'

'Is it okay to take photos?' I asked.

'Of course.'

'Thank you for coming,' she held out her hand. 'Let me know if there is anything else I can help you with. I look forward to receiving a copy of your book.'

Our silver service tea arrived with beautiful china cups and biscuits. Tarun was so impressed.

'Who would have thought that I would be having morning tea at the Taj Lake Palace?'

We took our time with our tea, enjoying the ambience of this magnificent place, and pretending that we were guests. Later, we wandered out onto the main outside area, all marble of course, where I recognised the turrets I had seen from afar. There was seating in two octagonal turrets.

'Imagine having dinner in there.' I told Tarun. 'I heard it was a popular place for wedding proposals.' I could imagine how romantic it would be at night with just the lights of the City Palace in the background. 'I must bring Bob here,' I told him. Tarun took my photo in one of the turrets.

Around the other side, looking out to Jag Mandir was the hotel's marble swimming pool. Udaipur is fortunate to be close to many marble quarries, and marble products are a huge export item from there.

'I remember this from *Octopussy,*' Tarun commented. We were both fairly quiet, each in our thoughts about the magnificence of this fairytale place. I imagined authors being inspired to write here—tales of times long past, maidens being rowed across the lake.

I had been to Udaivilas, the new luxury hotel on the banks of the lake, and it was indeed beautiful, but the history of the Lake Palace just added another layer to the romance, as well as the fact that it was surrounded by water.

Seated cross-legged in one of the bartizans, a barefooted young man, all in white except for a colourful turban, played the flute. Bougainvillea sprouting deep pink flowers wound their way around the columns.

I had heard a lot about the water lily pond and we found it in the central courtyard. Marble shapes of water lily leaves and flowers graced all sides of the pond. These seemed to float at the water level, with bowls of rose petals and golden marigolds filling the air with a sweet scent. I took a deep breath and sighed.

'What do you think?' I asked Tarun.

'Too beautiful for words,' was his reply. I was so happy that he had come with me. We took our time to wander and sit in the turrets and just take in the amazing atmosphere. Over on the ghats near Amet Haveli, the locals were bathing and doing their washing. The tourist boat that ferried people to Jag Mandir chugged past hardly raising a ripple. There were no noisy boats, jet skis or the like in Udaipur. The dull sound of a dog barking across the water faintly stirred the silence. There, one could just sit and gaze into nothingness, lost in thought, and this we did.

'I have to finish my book and come back,' I told Tarun as we caught the boat back to reality.

Taj Mahal, 2011

A few days later, I left by car for Agra and the Taj Mahal. Leaving was never easy. Udaipur was my second home. Taking a car saved all the waiting around at airports, and I discovered that by the time I added up all the taxi fees, the cost wasn't much higher. Tarun always made sure I got a good driver. Also, the baggage allowance on domestic flights in India is mostly 15–20 kilograms and sometimes—who am I kidding, change that to most times—my suitcases hit the scales at the maximum weight. I could pay excess baggage or I could drive in the comfort of an air-conditioned SUV and eventually be dropped off at Delhi International Airport by the same driver who had picked me up in Udaipur, without any hassles of lugging my valuable cargo all over the place. My allowance home from Delhi was 30 kilograms.

It suited me to be able to stop to take a photo whenever I liked, stop for chai or just sleep or read. I had never seen the Taj Mahal but decided that sunrise might be the best time, and stupidly thought that it might not be so crowded. I imagined myself standing outside in the dark, waiting for the gates to open. Would I be safe? Would I be there standing alone? It seemed a good idea to arrive the night before and stay somewhere close. I had not long checked into my hotel when my phone rang.

'Barbie?' It was a voice I did not recognise.

'Yes.'

'Hello. I am a friend of Tarun. I live in Agra. If you need anything, please call me.' My protective brother had been at it again.

'I'm going to Taj Mahal at sunrise. Do I need tickets beforehand?' I asked.

'Yes, my dear. You can buy at ticket office on the way. It is approximately one kilometre from Taj Mahal. No cars are allowed within the exclusion zone of one kilometre. From there you will take a motorised kart. Go early as there will be many people.'

'Okay, thank you so much.' This was all news to me and I was so appreciative.

So, next morning, I was on my way an hour before sunrise. It was only a couple of kilometres from my hotel, so I thought there would be heaps of time. The driver dropped me off at the ticket office and said he would wait in the car park for me. He said he would have a sleep, in preparation for the drive to Delhi. There was a queue for tickets and I purchased mine after around 15 minutes, and then was taken to the site in the train of motorised carts. I found out later that the exclusion zone was to protect the Taj Mahal from the pollution of car exhausts. I'm sure that this was a good idea when it was put in place many years ago, but from the haze I saw in the sky when I arrived the previous afternoon, I realised, there was still a huge environmental issue in Agra, as in most of the big cities.

In India, there is a story for everything, and the Taj Mahal is no different. I had spent my evening after dinner the previous night reading up on its history. In a land of arranged marriages and where women were 'seen and not heard', I found it intriguing that the Taj Mahal was built out of one man's grief over the death of his wife in the 1600s.

Shah Jahan built the now famous Taj Mahal to create an eternal monument to her. Situated on the banks of the Jamuna River, it took some ten years to complete. I had seen photos of it, and was keen to see if it would cast its spell over me as it had seemed to have done to tourists for centuries.

On arrival at the gate, I soon discovered that I would be less than alone in my viewing. The queue snaked its way around the turnstiles and I probably had at least a hundred people ahead of me. I was dying for a coffee, but was not game to leave my spot. Just as the sky began to lighten, the gates were open, and by the time the one hundred or so people ahead of me had passed their security check, the sun had definitely begun to rise above the horizon. I felt sorry for the poor young woman ahead of me who did not know about pre-purchasing a ticket, and was sent back to the ticket office.

Once inside the gate, the sight of this magical building was directly in front of me. It was certainly an imposing sight and in the early morning mist, the sunrise coloured the white marble with a wash of pale rose. I stood at the end of the reflection pool, seeing its perfect image on the water. How could one not be impressed by this?

As with many of India's historical landmarks, the upkeep is huge and I noticed the peeling surface on the bed of the reflection pool. But then again, that just made it even more special. There were people everywhere and it was virtually impossible to get a photo of the actual building by itself. However, for a price, there was a man who would clear the background for you while you took your photo.

I wandered around the wide balconies that overlooked the Jamuna River. Through the early morning fog, I could see men in small boats and others having their morning bath. I wondered whether they looked at it everyday in awe, or had it just become a part of the background of their life.

Large groups of monkeys ran along the balustrades of the balcony, looking to the tourists for food. There are no shoes allowed into the Taj Mahal itself, but there is an option of shoe or foot covers, or you can go barefoot. I found that there is something magical about walking barefoot on the marble surfaces of these places. I remember the temples I visited with Tarun on my first visit, and how tantalisingly cool the marble felt under my feet, and I could feel an energy that seemed to rise up through my body and left me with that feeling when your hair stands on end.

By buying a 'high end' ticket, the queue to get into the actual mausoleum didn't take as long as I thought, however as I looked across the courtyard, I could see the line for the cheaper tickets was perhaps 200 metres long. It was difficult to tell whether it was mist, cloud or pollution, but Taj Mahal seemed to be shrouded in a milky sky. I could see why it would have taken so long to build, as every post and pillar of marble was intricately carved. Looking out towards the river, the misty haze hung low in the sky and brought the Jamuna and the Taj Mahal together as one.

The Road to Jodhpur, 2013

Life back home went on as usual and I'm sure, friends must have gotten sick of hearing about my trips. I would come home on a high, that I extended as long as I possibly could, finding places in our home for the new pieces I had found on my trip, and continuing my habit of masala chai every morning until I ran out of supplies. By then, I would be planning my next trip.

It was 2013 and I returned to India once more. Again, Udaipur extended its enchantment over me. After heavy monsoonal rains, the lake was full to capacity and the daily activities of bathing and washing on the ghats had taken on a fun, playful air with shouts of laughter. Water truly was the life of this city—the Venice of the East.

'Lake is full. People are happy,' Tarun had said to me the day before when he picked me up from the airport. Now, sitting on my balcony, I could see it on the faces all around me. The summer rains had stripped the desert city of its suffocating, dusty coat, leaving the buildings and streets fresh and clean. The temperatures had dropped from devastatingly high 40s to just hot with the onset of autumn. Beyond the city, the surrounding Aravalli mountains were green with new growth. Udaipur sparkled.

Here, I felt relaxed and walking the markets was never boring. Familiar faces greeted me.

'Bar-ba-ra!' A young man called out from where he was seated on the doorway to his store.

'Aussie, you're back.' I followed the sound to the other side of the street.

'Remember me?'

I always answered 'yes' and smiled. The day before, a man had asked the same question, 'Remember me?'

'Of course.' He had looked vaguely familiar.

'Which hotel did you see me?' I could see it was important to him that I remembered.

His genuine smile prompted my memory. 'Kankawa? You made me that lovely chai.' His grin widened.

'You remember.' He put his hands together. 'Namaste.'

I guess we all like to think that people remember us. I had been coming to Udaipur once, sometimes twice a year now for the past eight years, and not a lot had changed. I slipped back into Udaipur as comfortably as into my favourite old sweater, embraced by its familiarity.

Further on, I saw a woman begging with a baby in arms. She laid the infant directly on the hot pavement of the footbridge that spanned the lake while she pursued the tourists, hand to mouth. The infant squinted its eyes against the brightness of the sun and the flies that circled overhead. I wanted to pick it up and hold it, but didn't dare. Its destiny had already been written. Seven years before, she also had a baby. He was now the young boy beside her with a plastic bag in hand, picking up rubbish from the road and begging. I gave him some coins. I saw how tourists dismissed them with as much consideration as a cow pat lying on the ground—something to be stepped over. Those same tourists who 'can't cope with the poverty'. How many times have I heard that! But having seen and recognised the same street people year after year, it was clear that their struggle to survive was ongoing and the sight of a tourist was a glimmer of hope for something, however small. Who could blame them? No matter how poor they are, we are still a guest in their country, and I try to remember that.

In the evening, I sat with Tarun and Shakti on the rooftop overlooking the Lake Palace. I could see the lights of the Monsoon Palace on the distant mountain, and hear the buzz of diners at the Ambrai restaurant directly opposite. Fireworks had been launched off the rooftops for a short period, and then it was quiet. A midnight blue sky with full moon and a sky full of stars made for a perfect evening. Sultry sitar music drifted in the breeze, and by candlelight we had dinner and drinks.

'We should go to Jodhpur while you are here,' Tarun suggested. 'We could take a driver.'

'I'd love to.'

'Manisha and Little Maharaja could come as well.'

'When should we go?'

'In a few days. I'll make some enquiries tomorrow.'

I thought about it as I drifted off to sleep that night. I was looking forward to spending some leisurely time with them.

After breakfast the next morning, I took a walk down by Gangaur Ghat. Locals were cooling off in the water and swimming across to the Maharana's dancing pavilion. I couldn't imagine what the water was like with green moss floating on top and goodness knows what else below, but at least it would have been cool. Others paddled on the edge under the shade of the mango trees.

I'd found that the nearby Jeels Coffee and Bakery had the best coffee and seated myself by the window overlooking the lake. The waiter turned on the overhead fan as he delivered my coffee. It circulated the already hot air around me. They did make good coffee, I thought as I took my first sip. Looking across to the other side of the lake, I could see that Udai Koti had grown from the first time I stayed there. It also looked as if the hotel next door was growing higher as well, chasing the view.

I had a little daily ritual. Each morning, I would take myself across to the Ambrai restaurant for breakfast. Sometimes I walked, but in the heat, I got a tuktuk. There was always something to look at. The day before, a man and his son came down to wash their goat on the steps. They pushed the unsuspecting animal into the water to wet it. A woman was on the step doing her laundry within a metre of them. After pulling it back out, they then proceeded to lather the goat with soap. The father held it still with a rope while instructing the young boy who covered every inch of its body in a mass of white froth. By this stage, it had cottoned on to what was happening, and when they tried to push it back in to rinse it off, there was no way that it was going to budge. All the pushing and pulling only created more resistance. Its legs stood firm. Finally, the father got behind it and gave an almighty shove. The woman doing her washing jumped when they pulled it back out again. It shook itself spraying water everywhere including on her and her washing. Maybe the goat was reconciled to its fate with the upcoming Muslim festival of Bakrid. I felt sorry for it.

It had been a busy morning at Amet Ghat. Earlier in the morning, there had been two women on the small platform, when another two arrived. Suddenly, all hell broke loose, as an argument erupted as to how much space each was allowed for their laundry. They screamed at each other, pointing to claim their spot on the small step. One woman picked up another's laundry and threw it to the other side. Furious, she raised her washing paddle above her head. Noticing my interest, the waiter came over and stood beside me.

'What are they saying?' I asked.

He smiled. 'You put your washing there. Not here. This is my place.'

They were so loud and certainly did not hold back as the screaming match continued. The waiter was laughing. There were lots of hand actions and washing paddles waving around. Finally, the younger two of the women got up and left. The older ones continued arguing, even though there was heaps of space for both of them to share.

The women sat with their backs to each other. One was in pink, a rather large lady who had faced away from me. Her broad backside was cushioned on the concrete step. She welded a hefty wallop with her washing paddle as half of her left buttock and leg hung in the water. Still sitting with their backs to each other, they continued to sling verbal abuses, their voices escalating in rhythm with the beat of their paddles.

A young man arrived. I thought, he might be the son of the larger woman. He gestured her to quieten down. He had no effect at all. Men who had been bathing further down began to gather around, amused by the argument. The son, embarrassed, rolled up his trousers and proceeded to hurry his mother, helping her with the laundry. She wasn't impressed and signalled for him to leave. Nevertheless, the two women continued to argue, almost matching their outbursts in time with the whacking of the clothes. The son's head lowered as the laughter increased. He then forcibly packed up his mother, placed the washing basket on her head and led her away. I thought he may have carried it for her, but he took off on his motorbike. She continued to screech as she walked off.

Even after she was gone, the remaining woman yelled unrelentingly to herself for a further ten minutes, venting her obvious anger, oblivious to her audience. Finally, the heat sapped her. Content with her laundry, she left and the lake became silent again, except for the sound of the water splashing on the ghats as a boat sent ripples across the water. Once again, peace settled on the lake.

Two men continued to bathe at the far end. The rooster of the Ambrai let out a long, loud crow. Strings of marigolds drifted by, remnants of the plaster Ganesh placed in the lake. The cock crowed again as the sun's haze continued to rise in the sky. I settled back in my chair, smiling to myself as I finished my breakfast.

Once back at the hotel, I showed Tarun and Shakti the video I had taken of the women. They could fully understand what the women were saying and thought it hilarious.

'I think the waiter gave you a "nice" translation of their words,' was all Tarun would say, rolling his eyes and winking at Shakti.

'We can go to Jodhpur tomorrow,' he said, changing the subject. 'We need to find accommodation. Come and look with me on the internet.'

We found a place called Ratan Vilas. 'I have booked a car and driver for the morning. We'll come and pick you up. Maybe 9 am. Is that okay?'

'Sure. What's happening at home today?'

'Everyone is busy, as Riya is getting ready for her Freshers' party at the university.' She had just begun an engineering course. The family was very proud of her. 'All the ladies are helping her with her dress.' He raised his eyebrows.

'Can I go and see her?'

'Yes, I will take you on my bike if you like.'

Riya was already dressed when we arrived. She had been to the parlour and her hair was long and straight. Her make-up was perfect.

'You look beautiful,' I told her. Her dress was a modern sari in pink, black and silver. She had added silver bracelets, a sparkling necklace and long earrings. Riya's friend arrived dressed in purple and looking equally beautiful—a pair of princesses. I took lots of photos.

Tarun took me back to the lake on his bike. The breeze was cooling on such a hot day. Some rain had reduced the temperature somewhat. I had dinner on the rooftop and then packed my bag for the next day's journey.

As promised, they arrived around 9 am the next morning. My heart sank when I saw the car. It was a small, four-door sedan. Tarun's knees were pressed up against the dash, and his head touched the roof. Manisha sat in the back with Little Maharaja on her lap, her legs pressed against the front seat. It would be six hours before we reached Jodhpur, and I was feeling claustrophobic before we started.

'Should we get a larger car?' I asked. I knew that from what I had witnessed in India, many people can and do fit into a small car. However, the temperature was still high and the sloping glass on the back of the vehicle would have the sun directly on our heads and backs. I was paying for the car, and for the little extra in Australian dollars, I would happily pay for a larger car. The other thing was that there were no seatbelts in the back. This happens a lot in India as the law only requires front seatbelts, so in many cases, the belts are removed from the back.

'Much more comfortable,' I have been told, but not if you have an accident.

'It has air conditioning.' Tarun tried to convince me. I didn't want to sound like it wasn't good enough.

'We have to drive past the rental place, so let's see how it goes to there.' Very diplomatic, Tarun.

As it turned out, the weather was hot but cloudy, and it began raining soon after we left.

'It'll be fine,' I told him, not knowing what else to say. Manisha was excited about the trip and I didn't want to do anything that might disrupt that.

One of my favourite Indian movies is *Mr and Mrs Iyer*. It was featured in the Sydney Film Festival some years back. It tells the story of a young Hindi Brahmin woman travelling alone on a bus with her baby when it is attacked by a group of extremists. She saves the life of a young Muslim photographer, also a passenger on the bus, by pretending that he is her husband. The road they were travelling on was treacherous, fraught with all sorts of perils. I had the feeling that we were travelling on a similar road.

'You cannot travel on this road after dark,' Tarun told me. 'Thieves come out of the jungle on the narrow passes and rob you.' Now he tells me. It started to feel even more like that road in the film. The vegetation was thick jungle with vines right up to the guide posts, where monkeys sat, unmindful of the car as we passed.

'There are tigers down there as well,' Tarun added. Just lovely, I thought.

During the day, we had to keep stopping as herds of hundreds of sheep and goats blocked the road. The tribal desert people were making their way to lower grounds before the onset of winter, along with their valuable animals. Camels decorated with strands of colourful pompoms and traditionally embroidered blankets, carried the tents and possessions. They were led by men, all in white with brilliant red turbans. Behind them followed the gypsy women who herded the sheep and goats into smaller, controllable groups. Bells hung from the skirts of these nomadic women, and jingled as they walked barefoot, while jewellery covered their arms and ankles.

'They do this every year before winter,' Tarun explained as goats crossed the road in front of us. Little Maharaja's eyes were full of awe. Like me, he had never seen such an amazing sight. I needn't have worried about him being bored. He was delightful and happily played all the same travelling games I had enjoyed with my sons on long journeys, when they were younger. However, I spy with my little eye, had worn a bit thin after a while. Every now and then he dozed off. Then, it was great to be able to have a decent chat to Manisha. Although we had known each other for some time now, I felt that I hadn't gotten to know her in any depth, as our conversations at the house were often cut short, just by the sheer number of people all talking at once.

'Poonam is my best friend,' she told me. How wonderful. The children were all like brothers and sisters. I liked the importance of family in India.

As we drove through each village, the children ran alongside the car, waving and laughing. Young boys flicked water at each other in the puddles left by the rain. I had flown to Jodhpur last time, and now realised the extremes of the landscape. We left the desert, then passed through a jungle to arrive at another desert. Every now and then, we would see a herd of goats, tended only by a young boy of six or younger, seemingly in the middle of nowhere. Responsibility is taken on at a young age here. Women walked barefoot along the edge of the road, their heads laden with kindling for the fire. Fields of yellow mustard flowers were dotted with the flowing scarves of women as they toiled in relentless heat picking the precious seeds. There was always something to see.

We arrived in Jodhpur in the afternoon and made our way to the hotel. It was good to be able to get out and stretch our legs. Ratan Vilas was a welcome surprise, a true heritage hotel with manicured garden and a swimming pool. Manisha was impressed. We were shown two rooms.

'You choose,' I told Manisha. One was a bit larger. 'Take the larger one if you like. There are three of you.' I knew she wouldn't pick it unless I suggested.

The rooms were lovely and as a bonus, the beds were soft and there was air conditioning. Wonderful.

In the evening, tables were set on the lawn beside the pool for dinner. Manisha had changed from her sari to a less formal outfit, and I could see that she was enjoying being away. She stretched her legs under the table, wriggling her toes on the soft lawn, and threw her head back to gaze at the moonlit sky. There was no grass back in Udaipur, and she normally spent dinner time in the kitchen preparing meals for everyone else.

Dinner was very tasty, and Little Maharaja used his pent-up energy from the trip dashing around the garden, only returning to the table when he needed another mouthful of food. It was relaxing and the night air was cool. There was no rush.

After a good night's sleep, we met up for breakfast. Once again, Manisha enjoyed being served her meal in the courtyard near our rooms.

After we checked out, Tarun suggested we visit Jodhpur's famous sweet shops where we bought heaps to take back to the family, as well as some to consume immediately. We spent the rest of the morning sightseeing around the city and Manisha took the opportunity to see some different shops. Little Maharaja got a new toy to play with on the way home. We left around lunchtime.

We needed to get going to get back along the winding road before dark and did not stop until around 4 pm, after we had passed through the jungle. Then we stopped at a roadhouse and had a snack. I was guided by Tarun as to what I should eat. The grounds were filled with custard apple trees and I wished I could have taken some home for my mother who loves them. I took a photo instead.

By the time we reached the gypsies, darkness was almost upon us. They had raised their nomadic tents by the side of the road. Campfires dotted the hillside. The sheep and cattle were huddled together in tight flocks under a shepherd's watchful eye, while the camels were tethered closer to their makeshift shelters. It began to drizzle and I thought of them and their children huddled together inside.

From there, it rained most of the way back to Udaipur and was well and truly dark by the time we arrived around 7 pm. It had been two long days in the car, and the little guy had gone to sleep.

They dropped me off at my hotel.

'See you tomorrow,' Tarun called.

I waved them goodbye, feeling a new closeness to him and his family.

The next morning, I had a little sleep-in. It was still raining, so I went across to the Ambrai in a tuktuk. The restaurant was quiet. A low mist hugged the surrounding mountains, and the white lake palace rose like a ghostly apparition amidst the grey.

There were no washerwomen. Too wet for washing to dry. On the far edge of the ghats, a group of young people were standing out in the rain, their arms outstretched, as if maximising the effects of the coolness of the rain on their bodies—rejoicing in it. I know when I was a child, I loved walking home from school in the rain. Nowadays, you don't often see people going for a walk in the rain. Many children miss that experience; parents fear them getting a cold or getting wet. I never understood the difference between standing in the rain and getting wet, and jumping into a pool.

Sadly, it was my last night in Udaipur. I was going to the family home for dinner and I wasn't looking forward to leaving. The stronger my connections became, the longer I wanted to stay.

Mahipal had come to the hotel in the afternoon. He was studying for an exam, or that's what he said anyway. He's a bit of a character and makes me smile. I asked Shakti if it was okay to take him for a hot chocolate. We walked to a place, not far away. He ordered a large piece of chocolate cake plus an iced chocolate, topped with cream and cocoa. There wasn't a lot of conversation but a lot of smiling. He managed to finish everything off, and then sat back and held his stomach—full.

Later, Tarun collected me on his motorbike just on dusk. It was busy time and I found it surprising just how many of the motorcyclists rode without headlights on. I knew the road now, and I was confident being a passenger on the back with Tarun.

As usual, when we arrived everyone spoke at once. I loved it. Little Maharaja looked for my iPad as he liked playing games on it. I was ushered into the front room where there was a brilliant orange and yellow tie-dyed sheet on the couch. I commented on it and everyone looked at each other and began to laugh.

'Am I missing something?' I asked.

'Riya made it. That is second attempt,' said Poonam, still laughing. 'Mahipal played a trick on Riya with the first one. He swapped the labels on yellow bottle of dye with the black one, and after all her hard work, she ended up with a black sheet.'

Mahipal looked sheepish.

'Take him back to Australia with you,' she said.

'Yes, take him,' pleaded Riya. He certainly gets himself into trouble.

Tarun's father Raj came out to say 'hello'. He still spoke very little English. He beckoned me to see his prayer room; I felt privileged as he was a man of few words. He showed me where he prayed each morning, and one by one, pointed and named the photos of the gods he worshipped on the wall. 'It's nice to have you at my house,' Tarun translated for me when we joined the family. I gave his father a hug. He's such a gentle man. When I thought about him and Mamma, I could understand from where Tarun inherited his gentle nature.

Deepak arrived for dinner as well. He and Tarun had been friends since school, and sometimes gave a hint as to the sort of things they had gotten up to together as young lads. Dinner was delicious and once it was finished, Little Maharaja jumped up onto the table beside his father.

'Bring Barbie to my house for coffee,' Deepak told Tarun. By that time, it was around 10 pm. Indians seem to eat late and go to bed late.

'Would you like to?' Tarun asked me.

'Sure.'

'Then we should go.'

We walked outside to the motorbikes. Tarun was already sitting on his bike with Little Maharaja in front of him. 'Hop on,' Tarun told me.

'What about the little guy?'

'He's coming as well.' So, on I got. I had thought that Tarun was just going to give Little Maharaja a ride to the corner and back before we left, but no. I couldn't see him as I was on the back, but I could hear his little voice. We were flying along the main road. Please God, keep him safe. The traffic had died down a bit, thank goodness.

Deepak's wife, Ursha and his daughter and son were waiting for us. She made us some delicious sweet coffee, and then showed me the artwork she does and sells—deities decorated with all manner of jewels and glitter. She gave me one as a gift.

We finished our coffee and Tarun looked at me. 'Chalo.' He went and got Little Maharaja, who had disappeared with Deepak's children. Then we were off again. Once again, I could only hear Maharaja's little voice at the front, chatting away nonstop. We dropped him off home and then Tarun took me back to the hotel.

'You have a beautiful family,' I told him.

'You will always be a part of it.' I knew that now.

It was a little cooler by then. The streets had quietened. I knew it was my last night in Udaipur but I would be back soon.

My green silk scarf flowed behind me and with the wind in my hair, I bid farewell to my dear Udaipur once again.

India via Azerbaijan, 2014

It was the end of May and summer in India had come early. Each day, the temperature rose to around 40 degrees. Usually, I would visit during the cooler months, but I happened to be on my way back from a painting symposium in Baku, Azerbaijan.

'Where's that?' you might ask, just as everyone else did when I told them my news. It had come as a complete surprise. To be honest, I had to get the atlas out to see where it was.

'Is it safe?' was Bob's first reaction, and that thought had also crossed my mind. The day I opened that email, I had no idea where it was or anything at all about the country. My ticket would allow me to do a side trip to India. There was double cause for excitement.

I had attended a painting symposium in Dubai back in 2007, and it appeared that the representative from Azerbaijan at that event, had nominated me to the selection committee. He was a young man named Adil, around the same age as my youngest son. During the event, he told me of the difficulties, as well as the cost in finding quality paints in his country, and so before I left Dubai, I gifted him the paints I had brought with me. He had been most appreciative. I had followed his progress as he successfully pursued what was not an easy career path.

As it turned out, I had been invited by the Azerbaijan government and so my visas, accommodation and everything else were organised for me by them. It was called the Maiden Tower Festival and each participant would be given a model of the Maiden Tower to paint in their own design. There was quite a bit of research to be done, and I quickly became knowledgeable about Baku, the Maiden Tower and the traditional culture of Azerbaijan. I found it fascinating.

The Maiden Tower is an ancient landmark, dating back to the fifth century and Zoroastrian times. UNESCO had named it a World Heritage Site along with other parts of the old city. Story had it that there was a man who was in love with his daughter and wanted to marry her. (It was the fifth century.) She, on the other hand, had somebody other than her father in mind for marriage. She told her father to build a tower, and then she would marry him. Knowing how long it would take, she thought he would change his mind. Alas, he did not. In sheer sadness, she threw herself off the top of the tower. Hence, the name 'Maiden Tower'.

That was the story I found on the history of the Maiden Tower, and I wondered if I would get the same story in 21st century Baku. It was interesting to learn that some of the first operas and ballets were also based on this story, but in recent times, there is no mention of the father, suggesting also that the age-old tale about their iconic tower, could probably do without the thought of incestuous goings on being the reason behind its construction.

The idea of the festival was that each participant be given a model of the Maiden Tower, 1 metre high by 2.5 metres diameter, and they then paint it in a design in their own style. There would be 27 artists from all over the world participating in the festival. I would be the Australian representative, and I needed to work out a design suitable for the model, and found it difficult to imagine reference to Australia on such a historical building. The tower looked like something out of the 'Rapunzel' fairytale. It was both beautiful and plain, being round with a wing that faced towards the equinox of the sun.

I researched more on the history of the tower and Baku, the capital of this oil-rich country. I came up with all sorts of ideas, and then read that, 'The Maiden Tower was the window to Baku.' With that in mind, I looked for ideas of windows, which took me to their traditional craft of Shabette—coloured glass windows set in timber. They looked similar to our lead lights. Azerbaijan was famous for this craft and in particular, in the Sheki Khan Palace. It had some of the most beautiful windows I had seen. I decided I wanted my tower to be like a series of windows and enlarged random shapes as if the viewer was stepping closer and seeing through the window. On the larger shapes, I painted scenes depicting the local history. On one remaining window, I painted my own tower, the Byron Bay Lighthouse, and signed my work there. This drew a curious interest from the locals.

I learnt that two other friends I had met in Dubai would be participating: Lydia from Canada and Amor from Tunisia. This gave me some reassurance.

Tarun was in constant touch. 'When are you coming? We are waiting for you.' I was looking forward to India, but first, I needed to concentrate on Azerbaijan.

A representative met me at Baku airport and drove me to my hotel, located within walking distance of the Maiden Tower. I was given a timetable of events and then left to discover the city, as painting did not commence until the following day.

Baku was like no other city I had been to and I was a little nervous. It is an oil-rich country and there are places where fires burn constantly as the oil and gas seeps out of the ground, hence the early days of fire worshiping.

I took a walk, and it wasn't long before I ran into my old friend Amor. I could see a hand waving to me in the distance as I strolled along the boardwalk, and then there he was. It was good to see him again.

We sat on a seat overlooking the Caspian Sea; Baku is located on its western shores. Azerbaijan is bordered by Georgia and Russia to the north, Iran to the south, Armenia to the south west, and an 8 kilometre border with Turkey to the north-west. I remembered reading in the newspapers, the sadness of 1990 in Baku when around 150 people had been killed in the streets, a time now referred to as 'Black January'. These days, Baku is 97 per cent Muslim but it is a secular state. Having read all this before I left, I was glad to know I had a few friends there.

'What are you going to paint?' I asked Amor.

'I'm not sure. I was so busy at the university before I left.' Amor is held in high esteem in the art faculty of the Tunis University. We had worked out in Dubai that we were born in the same year. He has a great sense of humour, and had told me his name was Amore, and I had wondered why I had gotten funny looks when I addressed him so— 'Amore' meaning love. We had a good laugh once I found out.

'What about you? What are you going to paint?'

I explained my plan. It was always good to run things by him.

Our first evening was spent in a rustic restaurant close to our hotel, the Shah Palace, with those who had already arrived. There was Nico from Greece, Roman and Shozanna, Igor and Tatiana, and Alec who was a three-dimensional pavement artist. Others were arriving in the morning.

We were very well looked after by our hosts, and spent the days painting within the walls of the old city, and the evenings dining in some of the best restaurants of Baku. The locals were very supportive and each day brought a crowd of people eager to see our work, and of course, our interpretation of their beloved tower. They found it hard to believe that I had come from Australia, and that I was painting their icons on my tower. With my blonde hair, they had presumed I was Russian. One little girl even brought her kitten wrapped in a blanket to show me. I found them to be very welcoming.

We had three to four days to complete our designs. At one stage, I regretted the complexity of my design.

I painted faster than ever before in order to complete it, impatiently moving the model by myself instead of waiting for the assistants provided, resulting in injuring my shoulder. Although I was aware of some pain, the extent of the damage was not realised until I was back home.

There was time in the evening to wander around the streets of the old city and venture into what would have been the original caravanserais, built to accommodate the travellers and their camels or horses. Now they housed restaurants and stores selling rugs and antiquities of the past. I could see a connection with India with some of the foods—dried fruits and spices, flat bread—and their rugs and textiles.

We were taken to the Heydar Aliyev Centre, an incredibly modern building designed by Iraqi-born British architect, Zaha Hadid, who was awarded the highest world award for her architecture. She was made a Dame by Queen Elizabeth II and dubbed the 'Queen of the curve' for her particular style.

We dined in tiny traditional restaurants where delicious flat bread was baked before our eyes in wood-fired ovens below the ground, to the most exquisite fine dining restaurants. It's a trip I won't forget. I still have the vision of two guys, sitting in the aisle of the bus, drinking vodka from another artist's shoe. My tower and I were featured in the magazine *BAKU,* published by Conde Naste's London office.

I sent photos to Tarun as I painted. The family was excited that I was coming back to India so soon. I left Baku exhausted but happy.

My return flight from Baku stopped in Dubai and from there to Delhi. I had organised my luggage to go directly to Delhi. During my stopover in Dubai, I had enquired as to whether my luggage could be further directed to Udaipur since Delhi was only a short stopover. I was told that it would be done. I should have known better, but took their word for it.On arrival in Delhi, I took my hand luggage and didn't bother going to the luggage carousel as I presumed everything had been forwarded on. I found myself a coffee shop and ordered some food. My phone rang. It was Tarun.

'Barbie, I've had a call from Delhi airport. You didn't collect your luggage.' Tarun was my contact number on my Indian visa.

'No, they said it would be forwarded on to Udaipur.'

'Well, the assistant airport manager says you must go and collect. Call him on this number.' I wrote it down and called him.

'Come now,' the airport official told me. 'I will wait for you.'

'Okay, that's no problem.' Or so I thought.

When I reached the entrance to the luggage area, a burly security policeman with a gun, refused me entry.

'But the assistant manager asked me to come to see him.'

'No!'

I phoned the airport official again. 'I can't get in,' I told him.

'I will come out.'

The security policeman stood firm.

'She needs to collect her baggage.'

'Cannot do.'

'How am I supposed to get my luggage?' I asked hoping a smile might help soften the situation. There was not an ounce of sympathy on his face.

'Ma'am, once you leave the area, you are not allowed back in.' Then, he gave his head a stern Indian waggle and straightened his gun. He addressed the airport official in the same robot-like manner. 'She cannot go in.'

'Wait here,' the assistant manager directed me back to my seat. 'I need to go back to my office.' He walked off flapping the paperwork in the air.

What was going to happen to my luggage? Time was ticking on and my flight to Udaipur was looming. I phoned Tarun.

'Did you get your luggage?'

'No. I'm still waiting.' I was exasperated. An hour and a half had passed. The airport official had come back a couple of times, but without any results with the security police. Meanwhile, I was imagining a black mark on my Indian visa in the future. Surely, I wasn't the first person to have this problem.

The assistant airport manager sat down beside me and gave a deep sigh.

'I just don't know what we can do,' he said. Up until then, I was okay, thinking that it would all resolve itself, but began to feel nervous. Had I committed an offence? All sorts of outcomes raced through my mind. Would I get my luggage back? Was it possible, I would be charged with some sort of misdemeanour?Just then, the lift opened and a man in a dark suit walked out. My companion almost fell over as he jumped up and ran to him. He was apparently, the head of the whole airport. My story was explained. They looked at the security policeman and then at me as they spoke.

The man in the suit walked over to the security police. I watched as the policemen once again shook his head, refusing access. The airport manager walked back to the guy who had been helping me, and there was more discussion. Finally, the airport manager went back to the policeman.

'I'll take responsibility. I'll sign for it,' the head guy insisted.

The policeman lowered his gun and nodded. It was done.

'Come with me quickly,' the assistant manager beckoned as if there was a chance the policeman might change his mind. He didn't need to tell me twice. By the time the dust had settled, my flight to Udaipur was ready for boarding.

Tarun phoned. 'Are you catching your flight or going to jail?' he laughed.

'I'm about to board.'

'Wonderful. I'm sending a car to the airport for you. It's busy here at the hotel. See you then.'

I had never been so pleased to get to Udaipur. My car was waiting. I could relax. I always loved the drive in from the airport. After Azerbaijan and Dubai, I felt like I was heading home. Tarun jumped up from his seat as I arrived at the hotel.

'Enough excitement for the day?' he asked giving me a hug.

'Enough.'

'Take a seat and I'll get you a chai.'

Udaipur, 2014

'I have a surprise for you,' Tarun told me as we finished the last of our chai.

I sat up in my seat. 'Tell me.'

'The rooftop restaurant has been built. Would you like to see?'

It had been his dream to have a restaurant overlooking the lake.

'There's still a bit of finishing off to do, but we can do breakfasts up here now,' he said as we continued up the spiral staircase.

'There's an extra level as well?' I could see the new guestrooms. In seven months, they had added another floor. Building in India is quick. 'The view is amazing.' He smiled. He was obviously very proud of how it was looking.

'Yes, I'm very happy. Look at the kitchen.'

There were marble bench tops, a big fridge and sink. Outside, there was an awning over part of the seating area, and the view was directly over the lake.

'Tomorrow night we will cook up here. Tonight, you can come to the house.'

'Tomorrow, I'll cook for everyone.' I was eager to do something for them.

'Good, I need some more recipes for the guests. Maybe, you have some suggestions.'

I liked the fact that he was asking for my advice.

'I have to go now, but you can come with me to the house when I leave here in about an hour. See you downstairs then.'

'You weren't wrong about the heat,' I said as I took a swig from my water bottle.

'Maybe, it will storm tonight.'

You know, I've never been in India when it's been seriously raining or storming. I don't care for electrical storms. I've read the statistics on how many people are killed by lightning strikes in this country—around 2500 per year. Then, there's those electrocuted when wires fall into the flood waters. And as if that's not enough, there's all the rats and snakes that get washed into the streets. Let's not think about it.

By the time I took a shower and changed, Tarun was ready to go.

'We'll take my bike.'

'Great.' The temperature was still high and there would at least be a breeze on the back of the motorbike. There was a drizzle of rain as we took off.

'Do you mind the rain?'

'Not at all.' We had only gone a short distance when the heavens opened and in no time, we were riding in torrential rain. Tarun stopped under an awning and we waited for the shower to ease. We were soaked to the skin. At least, it was cool. Soothing. The canvas awning filled with water and then overflowed at my feet. My shoes were sodden. I didn't care; it was refreshing. I love the way Indian people celebrate the rain.

Bob Marley once said that 'Some people feel the rain, others just get wet.' I could see the look of joy on the faces of the children as they splashed their way home; taking off their shoes and skipping through all the puddles.

The rain eased and we made a dash and arrived at the house absolutely dripping wet.

'Aigh, aigh, aigh!' Mamma laughed as we came through the door. Manisha ran for a towel. Cooking aromas wafted out from the kitchen.

'Come sit,' Manisha beckoned once I had dried off a bit. The children were around me and Little Maharaja on my lap in no time. He had grown so much and was a confident five-year-old.

Tarun reappeared in dry clothes. 'Much better,' he smiled. As they fussed over me with towels and laughter, I really felt like I was a part of the family. Everyone was keen to hear about my adventures in Azerbaijan and see my photos. It had been a long, exhausting day and Tarun took me back to the hotel in between the showers.

I slept well. It was still raining when I got up, so I took a tuktuk to Ambrai. The lake had fallen by about 1.2 metres since my October visit, but still reached the steps of the ghats. Bright green moss had gathered on the bottom steps. Children were playing with frisbees as they bathed. Here, they wash their clothes as they bathe in their underwear, and then leave the clothes on the steps to dry. Others were happy to put them on wet.

One little child had water wings on. I hadn't seen those since the boys were small. Reports of drowning in the lake were not uncommon. Others confidently dived in with the luxurious palace as their backdrop. Sometimes I felt like an intruder, having my chai whilst they bathed only 20 metres away, but they seemed to be oblivious.

There were two groups of men under crude shelters and a cloud of dust billowed above accompanied by a constant grinding noise. I realised they must be sculptors and I asked the waiter what they were working on.

'They are building a new garden there. Gate will close and people will not be able to bathe. Tourists say it is too dirty.' I felt sad for them.

Where will they go? It has been their bathing and clothes washing place for centuries, and now because the tourists want it clean, they have to go somewhere else.

As I left, I wandered down the path to where the gate would be. An old man was coming back after his bath. He held a cake of soap and a face washer in his hand and his towel hung over his arm. He smiled as he gestured for me to pass through the narrow opening first. I accepted and returned his smile.

'What is your good name?' he asked straightening his snow-white beard that hung to his chest.

'My name is Barbara.'

'And where are you from, Barbara?' He gave another wide smile. His oversized glasses seemed to sit a little crooked on his face and through them I could see his eyes, so dark they were almost black. There was a kindness that shone through.

'I'm from Australia. They tell me they are closing the lake for bathing.'

He nodded his head and looked to the ground.

'I don't think they should,' I told him, sensing that he was upset at the thought.

He grabbed my hand and gave me another big smile.

'Can I take your photo, Omar?' He nodded again and grinned as he stood upright and proud. His white hair and beard were gleaming. He looked cool and fresh yet he had just bathed in the lake where murky green moss covered the water's edge.

'Goodbye,' he said, waving to me as he left. I walked back to wait for my tuktuk. There was no rush. I wouldn't have met Omar if I had rushed off. When I first came to India, I probably wouldn't have even spoken to the likes of Omar. Most likely, I would have looked the other way when he smiled at me, pretended not to hear him speak, and hurried past him.

These days, I take my time. I don't rush. Yes, time to smell the roses—or cow dung. Whatever! How can you know a place if you don't know the people? Many times, we rush so fast to see everything, that we see nothing but the obvious and miss the hidden beauties. Like the day I met a young girl of around ten years of age who was selling small marble carvings down by Gangaur Ghat. Her mother sat on a cloth on the ground close by, but it was the daughter that was the salesperson. I bought a marble Ganesha from her.

'150 rupees,' she told me confidently. I paid her and as she wrapped it in a piece of old newspaper, I asked her 'What is your name?'

'Joshinda.' There was an arrogance about her. She stood tall, holding herself confidently. I wondered why she wasn't in school.

'How old are you, Joshinda?' She thought for a moment, and then went and asked her mother. 'Ten,' she rushed back to tell me, smiling and for a moment, dropping her guard. I gave her an extra 50 rupees and hoped she would be able to maintain her confidence with those tourists who would try to bargain her down. Her life was there making a living for her family. Such a load for a young girl. Her image stayed with me as I continued on my way.

I get all sorts of ideas as I wander around the old city. There are so many tiny havelis tucked away on the edge of the lake. One day, I would like to be able to buy one. Just a small one to renovate and make beautiful and maybe, rent out to travellers. It's a good place to daydream.

I returned to my room and the comfort of the air conditioning during the heat in the middle of the day, and in the afternoon ventured down to my friendly bookstore to see what the owner had on his shelves. I always seem to come home with more books, despite the fact I now have a Kindle. I like his store as he is a wealth of knowledge on all the books he sells. Books in India are cheap and I often find some new publications for four or five dollars. He pulled up a seat for me and gave me the rundown of what was new.

Once back at Pratap Bhawan, I took my gin and tonic to the rooftop to watch the sunset before Tarun and I left for dinner. Cooking in the new kitchen had been postponed for a night.

When we arrived at Ambrai, Tarun was immediately directed to the best table in the restaurant—a table overlooking the lake on the corner, where the view of the Lake Palace and City Palace could not be interrupted.

'Ambrai means mango tree, and that is the big shady tree in the middle of the restaurant,' he told me. At night, it was strung with lanterns and fairy lights. We ordered some chicken tikka masala, daal and rice. I ordered wine and Tarun had scotch.

'I was told today that soon they cannot bathe or do washing here on the ghats,' I said to him.

'Yes, there has been some controversy. You see, the lake is the main water supply for the city, and now some people use soap, and it contaminates the water.'

'Now I understand the reason.'

'Would you like to go to the Marigold Hotel again tomorrow? My friend tells me they have just finished the sequel to the first movie. Apparently, Richard Gere is in this one.'

'Oh, yes.'

The wind rustled through the mango tree and the air cooled. 'Maybe a storm will come after all,' Tarun looked towards the sky. 'It's almost the end of the season. Not so many tourists around. The group in the hotel is the last until after the monsoon.'

Back at the hotel, I had noticed that some of the rooftops were quiet, and others had already closed up. It's quite a revelation what you can see from up there. From Pratap Bhawan I could see some of the original homes that were quite run down. It must be intrusive for them to have the buildings growing around them. Every time I go, there are new rooftops clambering for a view. Floor by floor they climb. I *guess* there are engineers involved in all this construction. They reach for the heavens, devouring the view and sometimes their neighbours', and then they too reach higher.

The winds got stronger. It was inevitable. We finished our dinner and were ready to move should it begin to rain. Cloud covered the moon and stars. The wind picked up and as if by magic, the clouds disappeared and the moon rose, full and golden. The lights shone brightly again.

Next morning after breakfast, Tarun collected me for our trip to the Marigold Hotel, also known as Ravla Khempur. He had borrowed his friend's car for the trip. I was excited.

The horses were leaning over the wall when we arrived. The original movie was filmed in Jaipur and Udaipur as well as Ravla Khempur. However, the latest one was mostly filmed at the 'Marigold Hotel' and alterations had been made for the set.

Tarun's friend invited us for tea once again. They chatted on and I wandered around taking photos. It was a quiet, peaceful place. The surrounding village was small, but I heard that the actors and crew were generous with the locals. I found myself a place on the veranda and settled down in the cool with my diary and camera.

Tarun's friend decided to catch a lift back to Udaipur with us to visit his son. There's not much in the way of transport out there, so we had his company on the way back. I couldn't wait for the next movie to be released, and especially since I am a bit of a Richard Gere fan.

It was my turn to cook that night, and I had been planning a few things in my head.

'The cook will help you,' Tarun told me. 'He needs to see what to do.'

'Okay.'

'We need some snack type food.'

'I was thinking of some rosti-type potato cakes. They would go well with chutneys and sauces and could even be made up and frozen.' The other thing I thought of was hummus.

'What's hummus?'

'It's more a middle eastern dip, but would go well up here with vegetables.'

'I like the sound of that.'

I had sent the boys out shopping for the ingredients and wondered what they might bring back.

Unfortunately, McDonalds or its equivalent had made it to Udaipur when its new mall opened. Now, everyone liked fries, something not heard of before. They are now on the menu of most hotels and known as 'French Frites'.

Cooking was easy as the kitchen boys grated the potatoes and added a few ingredients of their own like chillies and onions. We ended up with really tasty rosti. It was hot in the new kitchen with everything happening at once. The new appetisers were tried with a very cold Kingfisher beer, and got the seal of approval.

The next day, Tarun arranged for his friend to come and read my palm. Apparently, he was very well respected in Udaipur for his ability. Some of his predictions scared me a little. He told me I would have a health problem, but I would come out of it okay. I had no idea of how accurate his predictions were nor how soon they would happen. He suggested I wear a ruby stone for protection.

Later that night, Tarun presented me with a tiny box. 'This is for you. It will protect you.' Inside was a beautiful, deep red ruby.

'You can have it made into a ring next time you come.'

I didn't know what to say.

'Carry it with you,' he told me. I hugged him.

'Thank you.'

This trip had been full of the unexpected. Firstly, the fact I was there so soon after my last visit was such a wonderful surprise. They say things happen for a reason, and at that time, I had no idea what those reasons were.

I had been away for a few weeks, so my time in Udaipur was short, but sweet. As usual, it was sad to leave, but we had been able to spend time together as it was the quiet time for the hotel.

'Next time you come, everything will be finished,' he told me as he waved me off at the airport.

Epilogue: Time to Say Goodbye

Dear Tarun,

My heart is broken. My sorrow is huge. I've come to Udaipur but you're not here. It's hard to face the reality. I knew I would have to actually be here before I could believe it.

Why do these things happen? Sometimes you meet someone, and you just know you will be friends for life. That's your destiny. But fate shows no mercy when it delivers its final blow. Life can be too short and death brings too many unanswered questions.

On my last visit, you gave me a ruby. 'It will keep you safe,' you told me. Before, I never needed the ruby; I always had you. You always made sure I was safe.

'Give her your best driver,' you would tell your friend Buphendra from the travel agency. Another time, I was all the way over in Agra, when my phone rang. 'You Barbara ma'am? I'm a friend of Tarun. I live here. Call me if you need anything.'

Coming back to Udaipur is not easy. I've brought my ruby with me.

When I arrived at the hotel and saw Shakti, we both cried. I feel bad that I am upsetting everyone, but I guess it is the initial reuniting without you that brings us to tears.

'It happened so quickly,' Shakti tells me as he shakes his head from side to side. 'There was no time to do anything. He was my brother, AND my best friend.'

I said nothing, watching his face as he struggled to continue. 'It was his heart,' he said, eventually. 'There was nothing we could do.' I hugged him. He looks so lost without you.

'We're glad you're here. You're part of our family.'

'Would you like your usual room?'

'Of course.'

There was a comfort in going to my room. I could feel your presence. I could imagine you nearby.

In the afternoon, I went out to your house. Mamma was waiting on the veranda when I arrived at the house. Her eyes said it all. She thumped her fist on her heart and tears rolled down her face. What could I say? She has lost you, her son—her beautiful son. And me, well I have lost my dearest Indian brother. She hugged me. I held her and we both sobbed. I cannot describe, but it stays with me still, the wounded, sad cry that Mamma's body expelled as we clung to each other. It was that animalistic, deep, haunting sound of a mother crying over her young when nature takes over and there is no control. It came from the depths of her soul. I can close my eyes and still hear it now. Never before have I felt such closeness without a common language except that of love.

You touched so many hearts, Tarun and to lose you so suddenly, in such an unexpected way, is hard to comprehend. Words failed me once again when I walked inside to Manisha. She looked tired and worn, and the sadness in her eyes was heartbreaking. I brought the last photo I had taken of the two of you and gave it to her. You were cupping her face in your hand, and you said, 'I love my wife. She's beautiful!' She held it to her chest.

Raj, your father, came out from his prayer room when he heard my voice. Those eyes of his—those soft, piercing dark eyes welled with tears. Do you remember the day I told you and Shakti that he had asked me to call him Raj? You both laughed so much, as no one called him that. He put his arms around me, and I could feel his frail frame shake.

I wanted to do something for your family but it was hard to know what to do. I made a photo book with all the photos I had taken of you, your family and me. Manisha loved it, as did Mamma and all the family. I also made a smaller one for both Rudrakshi and Deepak. I did not put words—just photos.

As we sat in the front room, the photo I took of you, looking so handsome in your suit with the red cravat, takes pride of place on the shelf with a candle beside. You were so proud when you drove us through the palace gates in your sparkling clean jeep with the roof off. I remember how we both met the Maharana and the Prince. We certainly had some adventures together.

Last night, there was so much going on in my head, I couldn't sleep. I got up early this morning and decided to go to the lake. I write this letter to you as I sit at Ambrai restaurant. I'm the first person here.

MY GOODNESS! A little squirrel has just come and tapped me on the shoulder. Gave me such a fright. I squealed. The whole restaurant looked at me to see what had happened.

I am thinking…maybe it is you, Tarun. Are you sitting up in the trees here at Ambrai, one of your favourite places, watching me have my breakfast, and seeing me sad? I think you are still here. Deepak said you were. I feel you have been waiting for me—waiting for me to say goodbye.

The lake is so peaceful this morning. There are bathers as usual but only one woman washing and the sounds of her slapping her clothes against the steps makes me feel cosy. A strange word to use, I know, but maybe it is comforting and a feeling of being home—my second home here in Udaipur.

The first boatload of tourists makes its way around the lake. The sky is hazy with hardly a cloud and the promise of a hot day. Now a little bird is making noises above me. Sounds like a baby in the nest is squawking for food.

Little Maharaja (I still call him that) was so quiet when I arrived at your house last night. Mamma said that he keeps on saying 'Daddy gone to Japan.' I guess, he remembers Shakti's trip to Japan. He must wonder at all the crying, and his Daddy not there. By the look on his face, I thought he might think that I knew where you were. I guess in his little world, that is his way of coping. He's only five. Once I gave Manisha the photo book, and he saw photos of you and him together, his smile came back, and he came to sit with me.

How you loved each other, you two! You would always say to me, 'He is such a naughty boy!' but you said it with such love, a big smile and with such pride.

I'm thinking of the squirrel again, and while I know I may be just imagining it, I can feel your presence so strongly in this place, and a little tap by the squirrel is maybe what I needed, just to tell me you are okay. I know you will be watching over your family, and me as well.

Our friendship is one that I could not have imagined. I know we got some strange looks at times when you introduced me as your sister. The blonde Aussie wasn't quite what anyone was expecting.

When I think of my brother Tarun, I think of a man who was humble and kind. You touched so many hearts in a life cut short. I must visit Sister Damian, and all the people at Asha Dham. They worshipped you. You were always there to help. I recall arriving on the back of your motorbike loaded up with bags—bags of tea and coffee, and biscuits. I had no hands to hold on, but I trusted you as you carefully manoeuvred the bike through the traffic. I remember the voices as we rode through the gate, 'Tarun! Tarun!'

I feel your spirit in the lake, in the gentle ripples of the water, in the splashing on the ghats, in the quiet sounds of the birds as they swoop low.

The palace is quiet. Remember the day I took you with me to the Lake Palace, after I had written to them about my book? I remember they showered us with rose petals as we arrived.

My book! I feel sad that you did not get to see it finished, but really there never was an ending. I just kept coming back, having adventures with you and your family. Really, I never wanted an end to my book. But now, I feel that this has brought me to a place where I must finish it. It is my tribute to you, because without you, my whole experience in India would have been over in one trip and not lasted the ten years it has done, or will continue. I would not have had the privilege of having you in my life.

I will always remember the times shared with you and your family. This will not be the end of my visits to India. I know that.

Acknowledgements

Of course, I could not have followed my dreams without the love and support of my dear husband, Bob. Thank you, Bob. Love you heaps. It was great to have you on my last trip to experience India and meet the people I so often speak of.

To my two sons, Chris and Tim and their partners, Erika and Maya, thank you also for your encouragement.

When Brigitte invited me on that first trip to India, back in March 2005, I had no idea of the magnitude of the journey that lay ahead. I loved India from the start, and as destiny would have it, met Tarun on my first day. Brigitte and I have travelled to India together many times since, and our trips are always full of excitement and the unknown. Thank you, Brigitte.

To Pam, my Scottish friend and neighbour—what a time we had together. We never needed to speak, we always knew what the other was thinking.

To my other friends who have also joined me at different times, Jocelyn, Wendy, Heidi, Marg, Carol, Lyn and Paul. I hope you also enjoyed your travels with me.

I'd been writing this book for quite a few years when I did a travel writing workshop with Dr Claire Scobie at the Byron Writers Festival in 2014. Some time later, I began a one-on-one mentorship with Claire. She is an amazing writer and teacher. Claire understood where I was coming from with my story and my friendship with Tarun. She taught me how to bring my book to life and gave me a confidence with my writing that I will be forever grateful for. Thank you, Claire.

Thank you to Dr Nirmal Kanti Bhattacharjee and Niyogi Books for accepting my mauscript for the Indian readers. A special thanks to my literary agent, Preeti Gill.